ESCAPE FROM THE ZONE

NISSA HARLOW

NIMBLE HOPE PUBLISHING

*For those who find their families
in the most unexpected of places.*

CHAPTER 1

ANOTHER ROOF

"You think too much," Viktor said. He tugged on the bungee cord looped around my waist. "Somebody's got to."

A smirk was all I got in response. I sighed and stared down at the backyard from my perch on the roof. It wasn't like the *actual* roof. Just a piece over the first storey of the house. Still. The last time I'd been up on a roof, things hadn't ended so well. But I wasn't about to launch myself over to another roof this time. If things went according to plan—and Viktor hadn't totally miscalculated—I wouldn't be leaving the roof at all.

Click peered up at us, shielding his eyes from the setting sun.

"Might want to stand back," I called down to him. "If Viktor lets go, I'll squish you."

"I'm not going to *drop* you," Viktor said, sounding

disgusted that I'd even suggest such a thing. I turned to him and raised my eyebrows.

"What if the cord is stretchier than you thought?"

"Then I guess you'll be going bungee jumping."

"Like hell I will."

He shrugged and adjusted his grip on the cord in his hands. The end he was holding had long since lost its hook, leaving a sort of frayed-looking bit to grasp. He did have it wrapped around his knuckles, but that didn't exactly reassure me. I looked down at the metal loop that was hooked around the cord itself.

"There've got to be better ways to do this."

"You couldn't think of any."

"I did!" I said, turning to him with a scowl. "You shot them all down."

He rolled his eyes. "Trying to startle someone who knows it's coming is harder than it sounds. Let's just try this, okay? Gotta get that adrenaline flowing."

"Niesha's not going to be happy."

"Which is why we're doing this here and not at home."

"You think this won't get back to her? This is one of her cache houses."

"And Xavi and Crystal are out on a run. Which is why we're doing this now. But if you don't hurry up—"

"Stop rushing me!"

He tugged on the cord again and pointed with his other hand toward the edge of the roof.

"Viktor . . ."

"You're all right. I promise."

"You can't promise that. You don't know how old this cord is, or if you'll be able to hold me if I slip, or—"

"You're all right *now*. In this moment."

"Yeah, well, this moment isn't going to last forever."

He sighed. "If you don't do it soon, we're going to lose the light. And if Niesha sees pinkhands flaring up on one of her roofs . . ."

"Isn't the point to *not* have that happen?"

"Yeah . . . but you're a slow learner."

I dared to sidle sideways so I was within whacking distance. The sound of my hand on his bare arm reverberated through the air.

"Hey! What's with the abuse?"

"It was your stupid idea. And it's not going to work."

"No? You don't think you can manage to not fall off a roof?"

"I don't think I can manage to not have my hands flare when my life is flashing before my eyes. We haven't all had years of practice like—" A squeak swallowed up the rest of my words as he reached out and gave my shoulder a gentle shove. Standing on a sloping roof just meant that gravity could have its way with me that much easier. I stumbled forward, watching in horror as the edge of the roof got way too close for comfort. I could barely feel the bungee cord around my waist, and, for one horrible moment, I thought Viktor must've dropped it. My body let out an involuntary screech as I planted my feet and tilted forward, out over the open space.

The bungee cut into my stomach, stopping my headlong pitch onto the lawn. I pinwheeled my arms, as if that might help propel me safely back onto the roof. My shoes were still on it, toes hanging over the gutter . . . but the rest of me felt like it was tipped out at a dangerous angle.

"I've got you," Viktor said. The pressure on my waist grew stronger, and I started to feel myself come back up to a less precarious position.

"You better, you asshole!" My whole body felt like it was vibrating. I sucked in a few quick breaths, unable to do much more than that thanks to the bungee cord. It was chafing my skin even through my shirt, and I didn't doubt I was going to have a nasty pink rash there later.

"No need for that sort of language," he said with a grunt as he pulled on the cord, tilting me back to a proper standing position. I threw my weight backward and landed hard on my butt. "See? You did it."

I didn't even dignify that with a response. Able to breathe freely, I sucked in massive gulps of air. I'd probably be belching later, but I didn't really care at that moment. Without looking at the guy who'd tried to push me off a roof, I turned and crawled back to the open window.

"Léa, I—"

"Shut. Up." I was shaking so badly that I sort of

dropped through the window and into the bedroom, landing on the blessedly soft carpet. I was halfway to the door when I heard him climb in after me.

"You did it."

I broke into a run. Thundering down the stairs, I clenched my fists. I could feel the energy starting to course through my arms, and that just made me even angrier. It was a vicious circle.

"Léa, will you slow down? I need to grab a few things so we have an excuse for—"

"You don't need me to babysit you." I stormed for the front door and wrenched it open. The sun had dipped below the trees, and the dusky shadows were starting to cool the evening. "Click!" I bellowed as I jumped down the front steps. "We're leaving now."

Click appeared at the gate, Buddy at his heels. He raised his eyebrows at me, and then, as he saw my taut posture, seemed to get it. He glanced back at the house.

"You don't need to have a tantrum," Viktor said from behind me. I stopped and spun around, only to find him standing on the stoop, arms folded. "If this is how you act when things go *right*, I'm not sure we should bring you with us for the escape attempt."

"You think that went *well*?" I asked in disbelief. "You nearly pushed me off a roof!"

"And your hands stayed . . . not pink."

As if in defiance, they rushed with heat. Viktor

looked down as an expression of dismay washed over his uneven features. "Do these look 'not pink' to you?" I asked, raising my hands up in front of me.

He shook his head. "Relax."

"I am relaxed!" I shouted.

"Looks like it."

"If the idea is to get me totally pissed off at you, it's working."

He sighed. "The idea is to get you used to letting things just roll off your back. Like a duck."

"Quack."

"Hardly." His mouth twisted in a smirk. "But you're doing better than you were. Your hands don't flare when you're startled. Now we just need to work on your anger issues."

"Yeah, well, good luck with that. I'm stuck with *you*."

He shrugged. "I'm growing on you," he said as he stepped back into the house through the still-open front door. "Admit it."

"Like fungus, maybe," I muttered. I looked away and found Click's gaze. He smiled knowingly. "You have my sympathy," I said. "Spending the last three years with that idiot. You must be exhausted."

He reached down to grab the grotty tennis ball that Buddy had just deposited at his sandalled feet.

"Don't bring that with us. It looks like it's carrying a million diseases."

He examined the ball, as if he might be able to see the diseases I was talking about, then tossed it back over the fence. Buddy immediately tried to follow, but was thwarted by the closed gate.

"Bah-dee," Click called in a sing-song tone, punctuating the dog's name with a familiar click. Buddy stopped and looked back, his tail wagging a little bit, as if he were unsure about this new game where his best friend threw balls into inaccessible locations.

"Got your dog?" Viktor asked, reappearing at the door with a small backpack slung over one shoulder. He closed the door and took the three porch steps in one jump.

"Got your excuses?" I asked him. He gave me a sideways glance out of his non-cloudy eye. "You know Niesha's going to suspect we were doing something she wouldn't approve of."

He shrugged as he walked past me toward the street. I turned and followed, glowering at his back.

CHAPTER 2

ANNOYANCES

Niesha was in the kitchen when we got home. Since she'd been living with us, that room had become the centre of our lives. I didn't mind; the basement was getting kind of smelly. But most of the comfortable furniture was down there, which meant that our time in the kitchen was mostly spent standing. Even to eat.

"How long does it take to grab a packet of mac and cheese?" she asked, her head in the fridge. She pulled back and glanced over at us, then frowned when she saw me. "What happened to you?"

"Nothing," Viktor said quickly, depositing the backpack on the counter. "Couldn't find any packets of mac and cheese. We could've waited around for your runners, but I knew Léa would be getting hangry."

She raised an eyebrow. "So what *did* you get?"

Tugging at the zipper, he smiled. Niesha and I

exchanged a look. "Ta-da!" He pulled out a couple of cans and brandished them in the air in front of him. Niesha let out a snort.

"Seriously?"

"What are they?" I asked. He turned one of them around until I could read the label. "Mac and cheese comes in a can?"

"It shouldn't," Niesha said. "I'm not eating those. *You* are not eating those. The last thing we need is food poisoning."

Viktor frowned as he placed the cans on the counter, then tapped his fingernails on the top of one. "What? They're not swollen."

"They've been in that place since I claimed it two years ago. And who knows how long they were there before that?"

"Yeah . . . and? Canned food doesn't go bad."

"Actually, it does. And faster than you'd think." She shook her head, sending her fluffy ponytail swinging. "I'd tell you to look it up, but . . ."

He sighed. "I miss the internet."

"Well, if our plan works, you can surf it all you like. Look up porn. Whatever."

With a mock gasp, he placed one hand on his chest. "I would *never*."

"Yeah. Sure." She reached for the backpack and pulled it closer. "Get anything else?"

"Just the breadcrumbs. But I don't see what good that does without the mac and cheese."

She sighed. "I'll have to think about it. We might be having rehydrated bread salad"—Viktor made a gagging noise that she chose to talk over—"again. Hey. If you don't like it, bring me something better. You had plenty of time to . . ." Trailing off, she looked at me again. I took a step back from the counter, feeling exposed. "What were you doing? And why are you all flushed?"

"It got warm out there," Viktor said. "And she wouldn't take off her jacket."

"Give me a break. It wasn't *that* warm." She narrowed her eyes. "Do I really want to know?"

"Probably not," I said. "But you don't have to worry, because I will not let *that* happen again."

She held up her hand and shook her head. "Okay. But you," she said, pointing at Viktor, "are on thin ice."

"Why? What did I do?"

"Are you going to tell me?"

"No . . . but that doesn't mean it was bad." He glanced at me. "Léa's progressing nicely."

"You're making me sound like I'm pregnant," I said.

He reached up to tighten his ponytail, grinning wickedly. "Not yet. That's phase two of the RZRA."

"The what?"

"Rift Zone Repopulation Agenda."

"Gross."

"I agree," Niesha said.

"I didn't say it had to be with me," he protested.

"It's gross because you're still a teenager, and

you're barely past the toddler stage in maturity your-self. We don't need one more creature to look after. So, cool it." She shook her head again with a frown. "Where're Click and Buddy?"

Viktor shrugged. "Outside, probably. You know Click and sunsets."

"Yeah. A connoisseur. Just like you, right?"

"I can appreciate beauty." He glanced back and forth between us. "How could I not, living amongst two such stunning—"

"Yeah, yeah, yeah." She shook her head and turned back to the fridge with a sigh. "I don't know what you were doing, but anything that requires this much flattery . . ."

"We were just working on the plan. *Your* plan," he added, raising one eyebrow. She turned to him so swiftly that her ponytail actually made a soft noise.

"What did you do to her?"

"*Nothing*," he said, waving his hand in my direc-tion. "See? She's fine. In mint condition."

"Nine toes is mint condition?" I asked.

"You only had nine when we met. You can't blame that on the events of this afternoon."

"Whatever." I shook my head and headed back to the window, which Viktor had left open. After climb-ing through, I walked slowly along the side of the house. As I rounded the corner of the porch, I spotted Click on the front walk, legs crossed as he sat on the cement, staring toward the west. My shoes made a bit of noise as I went down the steps, but he didn't turn. Buddy trotted up to me, dragging a stick that was easily three times as long as his entire body. I ignored him.

"Can't see much at this time of year," I observed, peering toward the west. The tree-lined street was awash in leafy umbrellas of shade. The only part of the sunset that was really visible was the twinkling golden glow between houses and trees as the sun slipped lower in the sky. The sidewalk wasn't that wide, so I settled myself down on the grass beside Click, hugging my knees.

We didn't say anything. We never really did, any time we were alone together. He wasn't a talker, and I never quite knew what to say to the guy. Getting stuck in the Rift Zone—in the town where I'd grown up— was bad enough. I couldn't even imagine what it must've been like for him, getting trapped in a place so far from home without any way to call his family and let them know he was okay.

"Are the sunsets nice where you're from?" I asked, watching Buddy drag his stupid stick around the yard like it was some sort of favoured stuffy. Click turned to me with a little smile and gave me a thumbs up. "Where *are* you from?" I asked.

He pointed in the direction of the setting sun.

"Really?" For some reason, I'd always assumed he was from Europe. Or the Middle East. Somewhere east of where we were, anyway. "What country?"

"Ree-fah."

"Never heard of it."

Leaning forward, he pressed his index finger against the cement, then began to drag it sideways in a jagged sort of line. I assumed he was drawing the outline of his country. He stopped and looked at me.

"Go on."

"Ree-fah."

"Yeah, you said that. But I've never—" The sudden metallic crash right behind my head made me break off with a shriek. Beside me, Click started to laugh. Though I was still spinning with panic and adrenaline, I somehow managed to realize what had just happened. I stood up like a shot and spun around, coming face to face with a grinning Viktor . . . who was holding a pot in one hand and a frying pan in the other. "What is your problem?" I yelled, still high on surprise. I wrenched the pan out of his hand and took a swing at him. He blocked the blow with his pot, sending another clang echoing through the evening. "Are you *trying* to give me a heart attack?"

"Whoa. Chill." He held his pot up like a shield as I feigned taking another swing. "I needed the element of surprise."

"I could've fried the other half of your face, asshole!"

"But you didn't." He angled his chin toward my right hand, which was still grasping the frying pan's handle. I blinked. There was no glow. There wasn't even any tingle. I felt my jaw drop a little. "See?" he said. "You're getting better. Last week, you would've been lobbing pinkballs at me."

"Stop calling them that."

"Why? That's what they are."

I let the pan fall to my side. "I cannot *wait* to do Niesha's plan," I muttered. His expression fell, just the tiniest bit. "What? You think I want to spend the rest of my life in here with you three?"

"Four," he said. "Don't forget Buddy."

"How could I forget the face-eating dog?"

"That was one time. You going to hold that against him forever?"

"Some mistakes are unforgettable."

His brow furrowed as if he were trying to make sense of my words. I stormed past him, still clutching the pan, and pounded up the porch steps. I'd almost made it around the corner when he spoke again.

"Let us know when dinner's ready, okay?"

I stopped in my tracks and spun around. "Are you fucking serious?"

"What?"

I marched back to the top of the steps so I could glare down at him. "Why do you always expect me and Niesha to do the cooking? You've got two hands. And you claim you're an excellent cook."

"I'm half blind."

"You should still be able to pour crap in a bowl."

"Is that what we're having? Crap in a bowl? I

mean . . . you may be a terrible cook, but I think you could do better than *that.*"

I clenched the handle of the pan so hard that it hurt. He was right there, and his head was an extremely tempting target. But I really didn't want to give him back the other half of his makeshift cymbals. My nerves had been jangled enough for one day.

"Léa, I'm kidding."

I blinked, pulling myself out of my fantasies of lobbing the pan at his head. He raised his eyebrows.

"You okay?"

"I thought the idea was to get me to *not* react," I said.

He frowned, confused. "Yeah . . . it is."

"So why do you keep pissing me off? You know I get pinkhands when I'm angry."

Pointing his finger at me, he grinned. "Exactly. You need more practice."

"I need practice in not startling. That's how they test for infection, right?"

He lowered his hand. "I thought you didn't believe in the virus theory."

"It doesn't matter what I believe. The people who'll be testing us might believe it. And if they think we're infected . . ."

"They won't. That's why we're doing this. That's why Niesha asked me to teach you guys how to—"

"What? Calm our minds? Let the Rift energy ground itself?" I shook my head. "I'm getting there. But you pissing me off is *not* helping."

"Anger does trigger pinkhands in some people."

"Me."

He shrugged. "Well, I didn't want to single you out, but . . ."

"You have an evil twin at the checkpoint or something? Because, unless you do, I'm pretty sure nobody there is going to try to intentionally piss me off."

"It's not intentional."

"And yet, it happens anyway." I gripped the handle harder. My hand felt hot, and when I looked down, I could see a faint pink aura licking over the surface of my skin. With a grunt of disgusted rage, I wound up and threw the stupid pan into the front yard. Viktor ducked, even though he didn't really need to, and watched the cookware disappear into an overgrown bush.

"Whoa."

"Shut up!" I said, pointing my finger—which was now flaring bright enough to be a flashlight—at him. "If this whole plan rests on me not getting angry, we're *never* getting out of here."

"So we don't get out of here," he said absently, then turned to frown up at me . . . and my glowing hand. "I get why Niesha wants to leave, after the house-burning and all. But is it really so bad here? We've got a house, we can usually find something to eat, and there are enough DVDs and games to last until the next apocalypse."

"It's not the setting that bothers me," I growled,

pulling my glowing fingers into fists and turning away. I stormed around the corner and headed for the open window. *It's the company,* I finished silently as I shook the glow from my hands so I could grasp the window frame and pull myself back inside.

CHAPTER 3

IN-FLOOR HEATING

bypassed the kitchen entirely and headed for the stairs. Taking them two at a time, I made my way to the second floor of the house, which was couched in shadows. But I knew my way around well enough that I didn't need light to see where I was going. I headed straight for the master bedroom.

Like I'd hoped when I'd first arrived, the en suite bathroom did have in-floor heating. There was nothing that felt nicer after a long day than taking off my jacket and jeans and just lying down on the tiles, letting the warmth soak into my bones. In the last few weeks, though, the weather had taken a turn, and the heat didn't feel all that great anymore. So instead of heading for the bathroom, I kicked my shoes off just inside the bedroom itself and padded over to the plush rug. I pulled off my jacket, tossed it aside, and lay down on the cushy surface, enjoying the snuggly feel of the pile on my bare arms.

Coming down off an adrenaline high sometimes made me a little drowsy. No sooner had I closed my eyes than I felt myself begin to tilt toward sleep. I tried to hang on to consciousness for a little while longer, attempting to use my annoyance as a stimulant by dredging up all the stupid shit Viktor had pulled that day, but eventually I just let go, allowing the still quiet of the empty room to swallow me up.

"Léa?"

I startled and blinked. Niesha stood over me, a plate in one hand, her eyebrows high. I struggled to sit up, rubbing the sleep from my eyes. "What time is it?"

"Seven-ish? I wasn't really paying attention." She held the plate out toward me. "Hungry?"

"Always." I took the plate and settled it on my lap. Four unevenly shaped crackers sat there, smeared with peanut butter.

"Sorry it's so little," she said, folding her legs to sit down beside the rug. She gestured to the plate. "Maybe if Viktor hadn't been so busy pushing you off a roof, he could've done what I asked him to do and gotten us some real food."

I froze, a cracker halfway to my mouth. "He told you about that?"

"Click told me," she said. "With a lot of hand gestures and a water bottle being pushed off the edge of the counter."

With a sigh, I set the cracker back on the plate. "I'm sorry."

She snorted. "You're not the one who's pushing people off roofs."

"Yeah, but I'm the *reason* he's pushing people off roofs." I stabbed my finger at the peanut butter, then licked the resulting smear. "I'm not getting there as fast as you. We could've done this by now if I wasn't so useless."

"Hey. Stop." She shook her head and leaned down a little, as if to catch my gaze. "It's not your fault."

"Maybe you guys should just go without me. I mean, I've been on my own before. It's not like I—"

"Nope. Not happening. We go together, or we don't go at all."

"But you *want* to go! Your parents are out there. Viktor's got a whole family waiting for his return. It's not the same for me."

"Why not?"

"I don't have a family out there."

She frowned. "There must be someone."

"I wouldn't know. I was raised by my grandparents, and they're gone now."

Her expression softened. "Are your parents still alive?"

"Hell if I know. They're obviously not interested in having a kid, though, since they haven't been around since I was a baby."

"I'm sorry."

"Don't be. Why would I want parents like that, anyway?" I pushed one of the crackers around on the plate, just for something to do. "If they're still alive, they're probably glad they were on the outside when the Rift happened."

She waited for me to say more, but I'd already said enough. The people who'd made me might technically have been my parents, but that didn't mean they'd done any parenting. Grandma and Grandpa hadn't talked much about them, either. I'd sometimes gotten the impression that Grandma was ashamed. Not that she'd had any reason to be; she and Grandpa had been my parents when the people with the actual titles had skipped out on their roles.

"I'm just saying," I went on, abandoning the plate and setting it beside me while licking another smear of peanut butter from my finger, "there's nothing for me out there. But there is for you guys. So I'm not going to hold it against you if you want to go now."

She shook her head. "We can wait."

"For how long? What if I never get the hang of it?"

"Viktor said you're already great with the startle reflex."

"No thanks to him."

She laughed softly. "Yeah, I heard. I wondered what he was up to when he took that pot and pan."

"But if I can't get a handle on my anger, I could jeopardize the whole thing."

"What makes you angry?"

"Viktor, mostly."

"Besides Viktor. Like I said, we're staying together. We're not ditching him, no matter how annoying he might be."

I shook my head. "Why can't he just be . . ." My musing trailed off. She grunted in amusement.

"He's a seventeen-year-old boy. How many of those do you know who are perfectly refined gentlemen?"

"He doesn't need to be a perfectly refined gentleman. He just needs to stop pissing me off so bad."

She tilted her head with a little smile. "You know he likes you, right?"

My eyes widened. "Fuck," I whispered. "Don't say that."

"What's so wrong with having people like you?"

"Nothing. But I don't need *him* liking me."

"Why not?"

"He's annoying."

"Besides that."

"Isn't that enough?"

She shook her head slowly. "Maybe, if he didn't have to try so hard, you wouldn't get so annoyed."

I gaped. "What's that supposed to mean? You think I should jump into bed with him or something?"

"God, no. I'm just saying . . . he tries hard. Maybe too hard, sometimes. And you push back just as hard."

"I don't need some lovesick boy panting all over me."

"He's not panting, Léa. Jesus. Don't be so dramatic." She leaned back on her hands with a deep sigh. "Maybe if you weren't always trying to run away, he wouldn't keep trying to follow."

"How am I trying to run away?"

"Metaphorically. Those comments about his face sure don't help."

My cheeks rushed with hot shame. "He makes comments about my toe all the time."

"You can hide your toe. He can't exactly hide his face."

"Not without looking like some weird-ass supervillain," I muttered. She shot me a dark look. "Okay, yeah, I heard it. Sorry."

"I bet he was a cute little kid," she said, her gaze drifting up to the darkened chandelier above our heads. "Before puberty got to him, anyway. He's still in that pool-noodle phase now. All limbs and greasy skin. But he'll grow out of that." She looked down at me. "What he's not going to grow out of is that scar. How do you think he feels when you keep reminding him?"

"He doesn't seem to care."

"Well, he does. You just don't see it because you usually look away after you make your comments."

I already knew that. She didn't have to remind me. A worm of guilt crawled its way up my spine, and I hunched over miserably, staring down at my bare feet. Nine toes. I shook my head and looked away, then felt a wave of annoyance as I realized I was doing exactly what Niesha said I always did. Again.

"Hey, Niesh!" Viktor shouted. It sounded like he was at the bottom of the stairs. "Is it safe to come up? Or are you guys having some sort of party in your panties?"

I looked at Niesha in exasperation. She smirked.

"Whether he'll grow out of *that* is anyone's guess," she said quietly. Then, turning toward the door, she shouted, "Don't you want to come find out?"

The next thing I heard was the thundering of his boots on the steps. His soles squeaked as he came to a quick stop in the doorway, and his expression fell when he saw us sitting there, both fully clothed.

"Aw."

Niesha laughed. "You really think we'd invite you to that kind of party?"

"A guy can dream." He let out a long-suffering sigh and leaned against the doorframe. "You going to eat those?" he asked, jutting his chin at the crackers. I grabbed the plate and pulled it close before he could get any ideas. Niesha stood up and headed for the door.

"When Léa's done eating, I want us all to do a meditation session together," she said, edging past him into the hallway. He frowned.

"Why?"

"Because you've jangled enough nerves for today. We all need to chill out and relax a bit."

He shrugged. "Whatever. But you better go let Click know before he goes to bed. You know he has the sleep habits of a senior."

"A high school senior?"

"I meant the old kind. But I guess either one works, depending on the time of day."

Niesha left then, and I took the opportunity to shove one of the crackers into my mouth. Viktor stood there for a few moments, watching me.

"You're not having any," I said around a mouthful. The combination of sticky peanut butter and dry cracker was almost more than I could take. I kept swirling the chewed-up bits around in my mouth, hoping to work up more saliva.

"You sure you don't want me to help you finish those off? You don't look like you're enjoying them."

"They're delicious," I said, popping another one into my mouth. He snorted as he pushed away from the doorframe and came closer. I was going to tell him not to sit down, but I didn't manage to get anything out before he'd already folded his long legs onto the floor, taking the spot Niesha had vacated. Damn dry crackers.

"I've been told I should apologize," he began. I raised my eyebrows but didn't say anything. My mouth was still occupied. "Yeah. Apparently, it's not polite to try to push your friend off a roof . . . even if there is a bungee cord around her waist."

I swallowed (with some difficulty) and shook my head. "Now you know."

"Okay. So . . . I'm sorry I tried to push you off a roof, even though there was a bungee cord around your waist."

"What kind of apology is that?"

He shrugged. His mouth was turned up on the undamaged side of his face, and he looked pretty damn pleased with himself for some reason.

"What's your problem?" I asked.

"Me?" He put a hand to his chest. "Nothing. Why?"

I frowned and turned back to my meagre dinner, snagging the largest of the unevenly sized crackers.

"I told Niesha we should try in a few days," he said. I nearly choked on my mouthful.

"You *what?*"

"If not in a few days, when?"

I stared at him in disbelief. "We're only going to get one shot at this. If I fuck it up . . ."

"You're not going to fart it up."

I shook my head, trying to dislodge his replacement words that were dangerously close to making me laugh. And this was definitely not a humorous situation. "I might. I don't have the control that you and Niesha have."

"Your control is good enough."

"You guys should just go without me," I said. "It would be less risky. If I fuck it up, they could deny *all* of you. At the very least, we should split up and—"

"Nope." He held up his hand to stop me, edging closer. I leaned back a little.

"What are you doing?"

"Your control is good enough," he said again, his voice soft. I met his gaze, focusing on his dark right eye. "They're testing for the startle reflex, not anger."

"How do you know? I thought your aunt and uncle dumped you in one of those group homes without any testing."

He shook his head. "They already knew I had pinkhands. There was no point in testing. But I know about the testing from some of the other kids who ended up in that heckhole with me."

"They failed the tests?"

"Obviously."

"So why do you think I'm going to be any different?"

"Because you've been training with me," he said with a haughty tilt of his head.

"You think you're some guru? You just made all that shit up. 'Ground the energy,'" I said, deepening my voice in an imitation of his. "'Feel the tingle move through you and discharge itself. Massage those pinkballs away.'"

He snorted so hard I thought he was going to choke. "Massage the pinkballs?"

"Your words, not mine."

"I can guarantee that I have never advocated the massaging of pinkballs." His eye took on a wicked glint. "Unless you're talking about—"

"Shut up."

"What?" he asked innocently. "You're not even going to let me finish my sentence?"

"Not *that* sentence."

He chuckled and casually reached for my last cracker. I grabbed his wrist.

"You want to lose your hand?"

"Sharing is caring."

"You didn't share yours with me."

"You were sulking up here."

I narrowed my eyes. "I wasn't sulking."

"No? Then what were you doing? The girl equivalent of massaging pinkballs?"

With a grunt of disgust, I let go of his wrist. But he didn't pull back. His body was still tilted toward me, and I realized how close he'd gotten. Almost too close for me to focus on his face. I held my breath, even as my mind shouted a warning: *Pull back now! Quick! Before he gets the wrong idea.*

A quick smile flashed across his features, and he leaned closer. My heart surged as I understood what he was about to do. A hot wave of anger slammed through my body. I reared back as my hand flew out.

The moment seemed to stand still as I realized two things: One, I was coursing with the fury of the sun. And, two, I was going to hit him. It was too late to stop.

The slap echoed in the empty room. He blinked and pulled back at the same time as I did, our movements mirroring each other. And I realized what I hadn't seen.

"Whoa," he breathed. He began to laugh, the sound a mixture of relief and amusement.

"What is *wrong* with you?" I shouted, my ebbing panic making me wild. "I could've fried your face!"

"Eh. That side's already ruined."

"That's not the point! Since when is it okay to go around kissing girls without their permission?"

His amusement disappeared so suddenly that I startled. "I didn't kiss you."

"You tried to."

"You *thought* I tried to." He reached up and tightened his ponytail, then stood, leaving me to gape after him.

"That was a test?" The words barely made it out of my mouth. A weird sense of disappointment crashed over me. I shook my head, willing it away. *What the fuck is wrong with you? Get a grip, Léa.*

"I told you your control was good enough." He paused in the doorway and gave me a little smile. "I wish you could believe in yourself the way we believe in you."

And then he was gone, his boots thudding down the stairs. I sighed and turned back to the remnants of my dinner. The last cracker felt like sawdust and grease in my mouth. But I ate the entire thing anyway, hoping it would give me the strength to face him later.

CHAPTER 4

GROUNDED

I had to admit, the meditation sessions were kind of nice. Not least because Viktor wasn't making smartass quips the whole time.

We stood in a loose circle in the backyard. Even Click joined us, though he didn't need to. I'd never seen his hands flare pink. Whether that was because he wasn't afflicted with pinkhands or because he just had amazing control, I didn't know. Niesha and Viktor didn't seem to know, either. But it was nice to have him join us. For the first time in years, I felt at home, and at ease, even though the undercurrent of annoyance was always just one stupid comment away. While we stood there, trying to synchronize our breathing, Buddy patrolled the perimeter of the yard, snuffling in the shadows. The meagre light from Niesha's phone, lying in the middle of our meditation circle, cast a feeble glow over everyone's faces. The effect was a bit creepy, especially on Viktor, who was standing across from me. I would've preferred it if he'd positioned himself somewhere else, even if that meant standing at my side. The way he kept trying to catch my gaze was starting to annoy me.

But, soon enough, he had us close our eyes and breathe deeply. "Into your feet" were his exact words, though I wasn't sure exactly what that was supposed to mean. I tried, anyway, imagining my breath coming in my nose, flowing into my lungs, and then oozing down through the rest of my body, straight into the ground. I wiggled my toes in the cool grass, listening to the slight rustle.

I couldn't hold my concentration for long, though. I never could. Eventually, my mind began to wander, and it walked straight back to my conversation with Niesha in the master bedroom. I felt my cheeks warm with shame as I remembered, thankful for the night air that immediately worked to cool them. *She might be right. I have been a bit of a bitch. He's just some poor kid who got maimed by this stupid town. By the stupid Rift.*

But do I really want to leave? What is there for me out there? Sure, Niesha said she'd help me get set up and find my own way, but . . . what if I can't do it? I know I can make it on my own here in Kenyonville. It sucks, but at least I know what kind of suckage it is. Out there . . . it could be anything.

Maybe I should just insist. No . . . Niesha's not going to let me. Then maybe I should just go with them and then come back. At least they won't be able to say I didn't try.

But if I do go with them and mess it up for everyone—

"Hey. No frowning."

I opened my eyes to see Viktor peering at me from across the circle, his cloudy eye almost seeming to glow in the phonelight. "I wasn't."

"Yeah, you were. Relax. This isn't supposed to be painful."

With a sigh, I readjusted my feet and shook my arms a little. Viktor smiled. I shot him a glare. It was like a reflex.

"I think we seriously need to make some plans," Niesha said, her eyes still closed. She brought the palms of her hands together for a moment, touching their edges to her forehead. When she opened her eyes, she looked a lot more relaxed than I felt.

"Um . . . session isn't over, Niesh."

"It's over. We need to talk about this." She sat down where she was, expecting us to do the same. Click followed without any more prompting. Viktor raised his eyebrows at me.

"You good?" he asked.

"Why wouldn't I be?" I snapped before I could catch myself. I sat down, folding my legs and tucking my toes under my knees.

"Still annoyed that I tried to push you off a roof?"

"You know why I'm pissed at you."

Niesha shook her head and held up her hand. Viktor let out a grunt as he let himself collapse onto the grass. "Enough. You guys can fight about it all you like once we get out of here."

"About that," I began, my voice hesitant. The three of them turned to look at me. Buddy just kept up his patrol. I licked my lips and took a deep breath. "Maybe I—"

"You're going," Niesha said. "We've already discussed this."

"I was just going to say that maybe I shouldn't go *with* you. Like . . . maybe I should go separately. Through another checkpoint."

"There's only the one that lets people in and out."

"If that," Viktor added. "I haven't heard of anyone coming or going in years. Have you?"

She turned to him with a frown. "I thought you were on board with this."

"I am! I'm just saying."

"Well, don't. We've got enough to worry about."

"I'd say the ability to get out of the Rift Zone kind of impacts your plan to, you know, get out of here."

She shook her head, sending her ponytail swaying. "We're going to operate as if we're getting out. If it turns out we can't get out via the checkpoint, we'll have to come up with another plan."

He snorted. "You going to tunnel out with a spoon?"

"Really? You think there aren't other ways out of this shithole?"

He sat up a little straighter. "Are there?"

"Of course there are. But I'm not about to share them with you," she said, holding up her hand to stop him before he could say anything. "I don't want you getting any ideas."

"Are you telling me that we could've left this place years ago?"

"You ready to sell your soul?"

He frowned. "What does that mean?"

"It means you're not a boss and you don't know the half of what goes on in this town." She shook her head again. "Never mind all that. We're trying the checkpoint, like we planned. We'll all go together"—she shot me a warning look—"and soon."

"When?"

"I was thinking the day after tomorrow."

"Why not tomorrow?"

She angled her head over to the side of the shadowy yard. When I turned to look, I saw Buddy lifting his leg on the headless gnome that stood at attention beside a frowsy-looking rosebush.

"Bah-dee," Click called, and the dog scampered over to him. Niesha sighed.

"We can't bring him with us. I'm sorry."

Click didn't say anything or make any sort of gestures to show he understood. He simply scooped the dog into his lap and began to massage his ears.

"Maybe we could . . ." Viktor said slowly. Niesha turned to him with a frown. "What? Dogs don't have pinkhands."

"They might be considered carriers."

He snorted. "Right. Don't you think this thing would've spread everywhere by now if animals could carry it? It's not like they've banned birds from coming and going." With a glance at Buddy curled up in Click's lap, he frowned. "Did your parents say anything about viral spread?"

"No. Everything sounded perfectly normal on their end. Whatever this is, it's confined to the Rift Zone."

"What if we spread it when we leave?" I asked slowly. Niesha shook her head.

"Nothing was spread during the evacuation, and all of those adults would've been exposed." She held up her index finger. "Reason number one why this probably isn't caused by a virus."

Viktor snorted. "Until someone gives me an explanation that makes more sense, I'm going with 'virus that causes superpowers.'"

"What superpower did you get?" I asked. "Being annoying?"

"Nah. Apparently, I've always had that."

Niesha grunted with laughter. But she sobered up pretty quickly and turned to Click. "We can't bring Buddy, though. Aside from the fact that they might not let him through, he could really cause problems for us. We're not going to have any money when we get out there, so we'll have to hitchhike. That'll be hard enough without finding someone willing to take a dog."

"He's not that big," Viktor said, watching Click's arms tighten around the animal. At last, he sighed. "You're right, though. So . . . what do we do with him? He won't last long on his own."

"I wasn't suggesting it." Niesha turned to me. "Do you think your vet friend would want a dog?"

I blinked. "Dr. Bryan? I . . . guess so."

"Good. Then Click can take him there tomorrow."

I looked over at the boy with the dog cradled in his lap. Despite the fact that he hadn't said anything about the plan, I knew he understood most of it. His posture was hunched as he sat with his head bent over the dog. A tear ran over his golden skin, glinting in the dim light. I wanted to protest again, to tell them I'd stay behind and take care of Buddy. But I knew Niesha had made up her mind. And I knew this was what had to be done.

"Dr. Bryan loves dogs," I told Click, who sniffed and dragged his wrist over his cheek. "I know you're going to miss him, but he'll have a great life here. I promise."

Click didn't move. I looked up, happening to catch Viktor's gaze as I did so. He gave me a little nod. I looked away quickly.

"Okay," Niesha said. "That's settled, then. We'll drop off the dog tomorrow. And then I need one of you to come with me on a run."

"With you?" Viktor said. "And what sort of occasion warrants the queen deigning to exit her throne room?"

She shot him a dirty look. "Are you serious?"

"Completely."

"I'm going to be leaving a territory without a boss.

Don't you think I should take care of that little detail before we go?"

"Oh. Yeah, that's probably a good idea. Wouldn't want a turf war to erupt once you abdicate."

"It might, anyway. But at least we won't be here to witness it." She stood up and bent down to swipe her phone off the grass. The light swung up and away, leaving my eyes to adjust to the darkness. Viktor was just a shadowy blob on the far side of the circle. "Let's make it an early night. We've got a lot to do tomorrow, and I want to make an early start."

CHAPTER 5

A NEW BOSS

"What if nobody's here?" I asked Niesha as we walked up the front sidewalk to one of her cache houses. It was only a couple of blocks away from Viktor's place, and I suspected you could see his bathroom light from one of the upper windows. The house was of a similar style to Niesha's old place, a newer sort of house that was built to look like an older style. The front door was painted a bright blue, a sharp contrast to the neon-pink tag fluttering on its surface. There was a bit of a breeze that morning, a lazy sort of breath that carried the faint scent of smoke. Either someone had had a campout . . . or another building had succumbed to flames.

"Then we'll wait. We've got some time." She paused at the base of the porch steps and peered up at the door. "That's why we're going tomorrow, not today."

With a sigh, I turned and looked toward the south.

Viktor and Click had headed off to see Dr. Bryan about an hour earlier, Buddy in tow. "I hope Click will be able to do it," I said.

"Do what? Give up the dog?"

I turned back to her with a frown. "He's pretty attached."

"I know he is. But he's a smart guy. He knows this is what needs to be done." She tilted her head, as if in thought. "You trust this vet of yours?"

"I don't have any reason not to."

"Then I'm sure Buddy will be fine." Turning, she started up the steps. I followed, slowly, planting my shoes on the wooden surfaces. I'd only been to that cache house once before, but I'd never gone inside. Viktor, Click, and I had simply gathered supplies from the locked storage around back. I was kind of expecting Niesha to knock on the door, but she just turned the knob and walked in. *Of course. Why wouldn't she? This is technically her house, too.*

I followed her inside, and she pushed the door closed behind me. I took a moment to look around. The place was sort of halfway between Viktor's and Niesha's, at least as far as furnishings were concerned. The living room had an easy chair and a coffee table, and there were pictures hanging on the walls. The built-in bookcases that lined one wall were mostly empty, though. Niesha started to kick off her shoes, then caught herself with a snort.

"Force of habit," she muttered before striding into

the house. "Katja's not a stickler about her floors like I was."

"They're still pretty clean," I said, staring at the light wood laminate. I couldn't really see much in the way of footprints or debris, so someone must've been doing some sort of housekeeping.

"Amazing, isn't it? Considering the number of people who come through here." She snorted. "What's Viktor's excuse?"

"He's just lazy."

She laughed. "I won't argue with that." She headed toward the back of the house, and I followed. We emerged into a kitchen that looked an awful lot like the one in Niesha's old place. Sunlight slanted in through the window over the sink. The basin was speckled with water droplets, as if it had been used pretty recently.

"Hey, boss," a voice said. My heart surged. A few weeks earlier, my hands would've flared as I spun around. But I managed to clamp down on my surprise. A young woman stood in the hallway, blocking the way back to the front door. She looked around my age, but with a haunted look in her light blue eyes that made me think she'd seen way too much. Her hair was straight and hung loose, coming just to her shoulders; a freshly dyed turquoise streak hung on one side of her face, while the rest of it was a natural blond. For a moment, I wondered where the hell someone would get hair dye after a magical apocalypse. Not that it really mattered.

"Hey," Niesha said, her voice easy and relaxed. "Where's Draven?"

"Out on a run. You need something?" The woman frowned, her fair eyebrows drawing together. "Did something happen to Viktor?"

Niesha shook her head. "He's otherwise occupied. And I need to talk to you."

"About what?" the woman asked. Her gaze flicked to me, then settled back on Niesha with a strange intensity.

"The future. Your future." Niesha sighed. "Look, I'll cut right to the chase here. We're leaving."

The woman's eyes widened, though it looked like she was trying hard not to react. "You're leaving? Why?"

"Because some pissy little king burned down my parents' house, and I've had enough of this shitshow. Haven't you?"

A strange expression flickered across the woman's features for a moment. But then it was gone. "Nobody's gotten out in a while," she said slowly. "And those people weren't part of Generation Rift."

Niesha snorted. "You make it sound like some weird demographic. It's not the whole generation that was affected."

"Might as well be. This is our town. Our life." She shrugged, trying to make it look careless, but I could tell she was struggling with something. She cast another quick glance over at me before focusing on Niesha once more. "When are you going?"

"Tomorrow."

"Shit."

"What?"

"You really think you can get out?"

"I think we have to try."

The woman shook her head. "Who's 'we'? You and Viktor and that mute kid?"

"He's not mute. But, yeah. Viktor, Click, and Léa"—she waved her hand in my direction—"are coming with me."

"What about your cache houses? You know, as soon as you leave, Xavi is going to declare himself boss."

"He can try," Niesha said, her tone dark. "But that's why I wanted to talk to you. And I hoped Draven would be here so we'd have at least one witness."

"A witness to what?" she asked, sounding suspicious, as if she thought Niesha might be about to take her out with a heinous display of pinkhands. But Niesha just smiled.

"I'm naming you my successor, Katja."

The woman blinked. She shook her head. Then she glanced at me again. Her eyes got a little shiny. "I can't."

"Yeah, you can," Niesha said. "You better. Because I don't want everything we've worked for for the last three years to fall into Xavi's hands. Do you?"

"You know that's the only reason he's stuck around, right? Waiting for his chance to take over from you."

"Like that was ever going to happen," Niesha muttered. "We've already got little boys running half this town. It's time to let the adults run this show."

"I'm only eighteen."

"So you should be able to handle a fifteen-year-old idiot, right?"

"If he decides to burn down my house, there isn't much I can do about it."

"Xavi's not stupid like Joshua. He's not going to burn down one of your houses just to be boss."

"I don't know. I wouldn't put it past him."

Niesha frowned. "So you *don't* want the job?"

Katja bit her lip. "I just don't understand why you want to leave. You really think things are any better out there? As soon as someone finds out you have pinkhands—"

"We've taken care of that."

Her eyes widened. "You've found a cure?"

"No. Well, not a cure so much as a . . . treatment."

Katja held up her hand with a shake of her head. "Save it. They don't work."

"Maybe this one does."

"None of them work," she said, her voice taking on a fierce edge. Niesha seemed taken aback, but she didn't push.

"Will you take the job?" she asked instead, and Katja lowered her hand, frowning. "You're pretty much my only option here. I know you can handle the distribution side of things. Xavi's out, obviously; he's too immature. Draven would probably eat everything in the cache if he were in charge of it."

"He basically does that, anyway," Katja said. Niesha grunted in amusement, and, for the first time, a tiny smile slipped across Katja's features.

"Crystal wouldn't want the job," Niesha went on. "She doesn't want the responsibility of making big decisions. Bryden loves going on runs, so he'd hate having to delegate to someone else."

"Bosses can go on runs," I said. She shook her head.

"Last time a boss did that, she got her house burned down." She sighed. "I'm sick of this life. I just want to get out of here. But I'm not leaving this territory without a decent boss. Life's hard enough in the Rift Zone without having to worry about tyrants." She raised her eyebrows at Katja. "So? What do you say?"

"You want me to be your heir?"

"No, because that kind of implies I'm going to die. Let's say successor."

Katja shook her head and took a step forward. "You won't be able to get out. Please . . . don't try."

"Why not? We've figured out how to get around the testing."

"If you don't . . . Niesha, if you don't do this exactly right, you could end up . . ."

"What? Right back here where we started?"

"No. Worse. You know whose territory you'll have to cross through, right?"

Niesha sighed. "At this point, I'm beyond caring. I'm

over it. If I die trying to get out of this place, fine. But . . . that's probably not going to happen." Her voice was tight, like she was thinking about something else. Worrying about something else. Whatever it was, though, she pushed it down with a shake of her head. "Life on the outside sounds pretty damn normal, and I've already wasted three years of my life in this hellhole."

Katja opened her mouth as if she were going to say something else, but closed it again. She could probably tell by the determined tone in Niesha's voice that there was going to be no stopping her. I watched the woman's body language as she seemed to sag a little, almost like she was carrying a new load on her shoulders.

"I know you can do this," Niesha said, stepping forward to lay her hands on the woman's arms. Katja raised her gaze, a façade of bravery glazed over her features. "The more Rifters on the outside, the better. One day, when we get this sorted out . . ."

"It can't be sorted out," Katja said, her voice almost a whisper. She looked desperately into Niesha's eyes. "Are you *sure* you want to do this?"

"It's not a matter of wanting anymore," Niesha said, pulling away. "Now it's about need."

—

The walk back to Viktor's house was pretty quiet. Niesha didn't seem inclined to talk, and I wasn't about to push her. She'd just made a huge move, and I wasn't sure what she was feeling. Relief? Regret? Honestly, if it had been me, I probably would've been feeling a hell of a lot of remorse at that moment. And when I realized why, I felt the weight of what we were about to attempt crash over me.

"If we can't get out," I said slowly, folding my arms across my chest as if to shield myself from the thought, "you're going to have nothing to come back to."

She sighed. "I know."

"Are you okay with that? You might not like being a boss, but *not* being a boss is worse."

"Depends on your perspective." She tipped her head back to stare up at the tree branches that arched overhead. "Being in charge can be exhausting."

"So can being bossed around by a kid on an ego trip."

"Katja's not like that. Which is why I picked her."

"Would she give you back the job if you asked?"

"Probably. But I wouldn't ask." She lowered her gaze and turned to me. "The only reason I'm a boss in the first place is because I was taking care of my parents' house. I was technically an adult when the Rift happened, so I was allowed to stay on my own."

"So you were an adult with a house. That makes a boss?"

She grunted. "On this side of town, it did. Not to sound privileged or anything, but people around here never had to fight for every scrap. That's why things are so much rougher in other parts of town. The people who ended up as bosses there . . . well, they didn't just fall into the job like I did. They had to take it. Sometimes with force."

I shuddered and tightened my arms.

"If we don't make it out, we'll come back here. I'm not going to ask Katja to give up her new job—that wouldn't be right, or fair—but she wouldn't kick us out of her territory, that's for sure."

"She wouldn't kick *you* out of it," I said, the words already out before I could stop them. But instead of the confusion I expected, there was just a nod.

"Yeah, I know."

"Do you like her?"

"It's more complicated than that. There's the age thing—"

"What? Four years?"

"That's a lot, especially at our age."

"She's more mature than Viktor."

She laughed. "Everybody's more mature than Viktor. But," she said, her voice getting serious once more, "there's also the power imbalance. There's *still* a power imbalance. Bosses can't get involved like that."

"They do, though."

"Well, they shouldn't." She shook her head. "It probably wouldn't be an issue with Katja, but still. Remember, we live in the Rift Zone. You don't want to have too many things in your life that can be leveraged against you."

"Like girlfriends?"

"Girlfriends. Boyfriends. Dogs. Houses."

I stared down at the sidewalk in front of us. "What about regular friends?"

"A necessary evil." She sighed. "I'm not going to be naïve about it. And I know what I said to Viktor outside Joshua's store a few weeks ago. But I also know that surviving without anyone on your side is just that: surviving. And I'm tired of doing that. Aren't you?"

"Tired of surviving? Not really."

She smiled. "No, I meant surviving as opposed to living. It's been three years since I was allowed to *live*. That's long enough . . . don't you think?"

CHAPTER 6

BORDERLINE

I didn't sleep well that night. Nobody did. There was a current of nervousness that ran through the house, almost visible like the pink energy that ran over my hands when I got pissed off at Viktor. It didn't help that Click was miserable. He didn't speak, even to utter Buddy's name, but we all knew why he was upset. When we went to bed, he curled up on his side, hugging a wad of blankets. Viktor tried to cheer him up with some of that crap purple licorice in the basement's stash of junk food. It didn't work.

Niesha was up before dawn, prowling around the basement in the dark. She didn't use her phone for light, though whether that was so she wouldn't wake us or she was charging the battery one last time before our trip, I wasn't sure. I pretended she hadn't woken me when she got out of bed, and I closed my eyes again, hoping to get a little more sleep. But my mind was whirling, and I almost couldn't keep my eyes closed.

Conflicting emotions roiled through me. I couldn't even put my finger on most of them, but there were a few that stood out well enough: nervousness, fear, uncertainty. I still wasn't entirely sure that Niesha was right about needing people. I'd done just fine on my own, hadn't I? Well, except for the toe thing. But, technically, that had happened when I'd been stupid enough to trust that other people gave a shit about me at all, so . . .

"Planning on leaving without us?" Viktor's sleepy voice said. I heard a small grunt come from the direction of one of the couches, where a vague shadow was moving about.

"Why would I do that? You think the Rift Zone wants your sorry ass around any longer than necessary? This mission is for the good of everyone in Kenyonville."

Viktor chuckled, then made a sort of squeaky noise as if he were stretching. A moment later, a pink light flared, illuminating the room in a freakish glow. I could see Niesha's frown as she whirled to face him.

"Put that out."

"Why?"

"Because if you hurt yourself, we won't be going. I don't want any delays."

He snorted, but he held his hand a little farther away from his body. "You think I can't handle my own pinkhands?"

"Ask your face."

"Touché."

She shook her head and turned back to the piles on the couch. We'd taken to tossing our clothes there when we weren't wearing them, so I figured she was getting dressed. "Get up. Pee. Shower. Do whatever you need to do. I want to get out of here before seven."

"Nobody told me a shower was required."

"Do you enjoy your own stink or something?"

"No."

"Then I don't understand the aversion to soap and water."

"It's not the soap. The water's *cold*," he said, his voice tipping way too close to a whine. Niesha sighed.

"Fine. Don't shower. But if the soldiers at the checkpoint won't let you pass because they think you're some sort of biohazard . . ."

"Hey! I'm not a biohazard."

"You smell like one."

"BO is not a biohazard." He swung his long legs off the bed, still holding his glowing hand out to one side. When he was standing, he paused and shone the light toward Click, who was curled up in much the same position as the night before. "C'mon, Click. Rise and shine."

A moment later, Click uncurled himself and sat up. When he caught my gaze in the dim pink light, I almost sucked in a breath. His sadness was so complete, it was radiating off him, more potent than anything Viktor's armpits could've produced.

"Dr. Bryan loves dogs," I said hesitantly, not at all sure what I could say that would . . . well, not make him feel *better*, but maybe reassure him.

"He should," Niesha said. "He is a vet, after all."

"We've got his address," I went on, staring at Click, who'd moved his gaze down to his feet. "Once we're out, and you've gone home, you can send him a letter."

"How?" Viktor asked. "Don't get his hopes up if—"

"He can send it to a checkpoint." I turned back to Click. "You can ask about Buddy. I'm sure Dr. Bryan would give you an update."

Click said nothing. Niesha sighed.

"Viktor, bathroom. Now."

"I'm not—"

"Jesus. Just pee, will you? I don't want to listen to you whine when you have to go after the first five minutes."

"Yes, Mom." He rolled his eyes and stalked to the door, taking the light with him. Niesha grunted, and her shadow shook its head.

"Just a few more hours," she muttered as if trying to give herself strength. "You can do it."

But there was a distinct sadness in her tone that made me think she wasn't as eager to get rid of Viktor as she pretended to be.

—

A few hours later, the four of us stood on the sidewalk, staring toward the west. The day was already warm, but I still shivered as I stared at the messy pink line that had been spray-painted right down the centre of the asphalt. The far side of the street didn't look that different, but there was a weird energy that seemed to emanate from that direction, raising the hairs on the back of my neck. It was probably all in my imagination . . . but the others must've felt it, too. Which was why we were just standing there.

"Now what?" Viktor asked. "You expect us to fly?"

Niesha snorted. "Like that would do much good. They've got guns."

"So do Joshua's goons," I pointed out. She shook her head.

"They have pellet guns." Turning to me, she frowned. "You didn't think those were real, did you?"

I shrugged.

"They looked pretty real," Viktor said. I glanced at him, grateful that I wasn't the only idiot in the group who hadn't noticed.

"That's the idea." Niesha adjusted the backpack slung on her shoulders. "But we're not going to be that lucky with Marc's guys. They're armed, and they're not afraid to use the weapons they've got."

I swallowed hard and willed myself to keep my feet planted on the sidewalk. All I wanted to do was turn and run. Back to Viktor's house. Back to the smelly basement with the crappy snacks and the stupid DVDs and a dog that farted too much. I chewed on my lip, trying to think of something I could say that would make that scenario a reality. On my right, Viktor shifted. I didn't realize what he was doing until I felt his hand slip into mine.

My first instinct was to startle and pull away. Luckily, I managed not to fry his hand as I turned to him with a glare.

"What the fuck do you think you're doing?"

He blinked. "Reassuring you?"

I wrenched my hand away. He shrugged, trying to make it look careless, but I could tell he was a bit stung. He kept the ruined side of his face toward me, probably so I wouldn't see his expression.

"Knock it off," Niesha said, drawing my attention her way. She frowned across the street, her gaze distant. "We don't want to draw too much attention. If we stick to the streets and make it look like we belong in the territory, we can probably make it through there unaccosted. But if you two are—"

"Don't blame me!" I said. "He started it."

"Yeah. I started it. I was trying to make you feel better. So sorry. I won't do it again."

"You better not."

His jaw clenched. "Bunny."

"Shut up!"

"You shut up," he mumbled.

"I'll shut up if you grow up." I glared at him for a

moment. His jaw was tight. His whole body was. He wore that tension like clothes he'd outgrown months earlier: awkwardly. "You're scared shitless. I get it. But you don't have to take it out on me."

He folded his arms. But some of the tension in his body seemed to ease, almost as if me pointing out his fear had helped to dissipate it.

"Maybe you should meditate," I suggested.

"I'd have to close my eyes."

"So?"

"How would I see danger coming?"

"It doesn't matter either way. You could see a grizzly bear charging at you, and you'd probably try to tell it a joke."

"Are you saying I'm useless in a crisis?" he asked, a hint of familiar cheekiness creeping back into his tone.

"Enough." Niesha peered past me to fix him with a glare. "Do you not want to go or something?"

"Why do you say that?"

"We'd be a few blocks closer to the checkpoint by now if you weren't bitching so hard."

"I'm not bunnying."

"It almost seems like you'd rather stay here."

"I don't want to stay *here*. I mean, the street does have a pretty pink line for decor, but—"

"Jesus." She pressed her fingers to her forehead with a suffering sigh. "Let's just get through Marc's territory and make it through the checkpoint. And then you two can ramp up this lovers' quarrel all you like."

"We're not lovers," I snapped.

Viktor snorted. I narrowed my eyes at him, but he wouldn't even look at me. Instead, he let his arms fall as he stepped off the curb and strolled into the street, heading toward the pink line. Niesha hissed and waved her hand. He turned but didn't stop, continuing to walk backward.

"What?"

"We're not done here."

He shuffled to a stop, rolling his eyes. "I thought you wanted to get out of here today."

"I do. Which is why we need to have some ground rules."

Rubbing his hands together, he grinned. "Oh, goody!"

"Just shut up and listen, will you?" She looked at me and Click, then turned back to Viktor. "We stay quiet until we're out of Marc's territory. No talking."

"You don't think that'll look a little suspicious?"

"No questions," she snapped, fixing him with a pretty intense gaze. He blinked and backed up a step.

"Whoa, there, Miss Dictator."

"You can thank me later, once we've made it through without any incidents."

"What kind of incidents do you think we're going to have?"

"Hell if I know. With you, it could be anything. You might decide to lob a Riftball at someone."

"Only if they throw one at me first."

"You might piss on someone's fence."

"Excuse me?"

"It wouldn't be the first time."

He coughed indignantly. "I went before we left. Like you ordered me to."

"Good. Then you *do* know how to follow directions."

He just raised his eyebrows at her and waved his hand. "Continue."

"Keep to the middle of the street. Stay away from anything that looks like it might be an asset: buildings, cars, whatever. I don't want to give him any excuse to come after us."

"This is Permanent Marc we're talking about here. Since when does he need an excuse? The guy's a farting psychopath."

She jabbed her finger in his direction, her eyes wide. "That," she said, "is exactly what I'm talking about. Will you shut your mouth before you get us all killed?"

He shook his head and turned to look into the territory. "We're probably blocks from the creep's nest. He's not going to live right on the border. I think we're safe."

"You think he doesn't have runners with ears?"

He turned back, looking a little pale. Niesha sighed and stepped off the curb to join him in the street. "Just keep your mouth shut, and we'll be fine."

Click followed them, but I stayed where I was. I tipped my head back, staring up at the sky, and tried to focus on the fluffy white clouds above us. Anything to push away the memories that had started to crowd my head the moment I'd seen that painted line. My hands felt hot, but I automatically pushed the energy down toward my feet, barely even thinking about it. I rubbed my sweaty palms on my jeans and swallowed hard.

I can't do this. I can't let them walk through there, either. What if . . . ? No. It's fine. Relax. Nothing's going to happen to them. Especially if I'm not there, freaking out. I can just turn around and head back to the house. Niesha won't risk calling out to me. Not here. Not if she values—

"Léa," Viktor whispered. As I lowered my gaze, he stepped into it. His eyebrows were drawn together, and the expression on his face was so far from the usual lightness that it looked . . . weird.

"I can't," I said. His frown deepened. "You guys need to go on without me. I . . ."

"You don't want to get out of here?"

"What is there for me out there? I'm better off staying."

"By yourself." It wasn't a question. I shrugged. "You know you're part of our crew, right?"

I screwed up my nose. "Your crew?"

"Yeah. Rescuing face-eating dogs. Trafficking Cheeznudles. Throwing pinkballs. Saving the world."

"How are we saving the world?"

"Eh . . . I'm still figuring that part out." The intact side of his face rose in a little smile. "But I do know that it requires four people. So you have to come with us. Otherwise, we'll have to find someone else, and that'll involve holding auditions, which will take too long, and then Niesha will get all weird and start using her favourite words, which I'll have to translate."

"I didn't have to audition."

"'Cause we already knew you were a perfect fit." He tilted his head toward Niesha and Click, who were waiting quietly, just watching. Maybe listening. I looked back at Viktor. He held out his hand like he wanted me to take it. I just stared at his long fingers for a moment, trying to think up another excuse. Anything would've done, really. But my brain didn't seem to want to cooperate.

So I slapped my hand into his and gave it a rough squeeze. He let out a grunt of surprised laughter. I dug my nails into his hand.

But I didn't let go as he led me off the sidewalk and over the painted line. It was kind of reassuring to hold on to something, considering I was freaking out a bit. It was also super satisfying to know that I'd confused the hell out of him. So I kept my hand firmly clamped around his as the four of us marched into Permanent Marc's territory.

CHAPTER 7

ENEMY TERRITORY

By the time we were halfway to the checkpoint, I was not only tired of the silence, but I was longing to hear Viktor's stupid comments. I had to settle for just holding his hand. I gave up trying to hurt him with my nails, reasoning that I could always correct any misunderstandings later if he happened to get the wrong idea. It was kind of nice, though; I'd never held a guy's hand before, and it was just the thing I needed as we brazenly walked through the territory of one of the most notorious bosses in the Rift Zone.

Realistically, Niesha's presence was probably more of a danger than mine. If I freaked out, it would draw attention, sure. But if someone realized another boss was prowling around in Permanent Marc's territory, and that got back to him . . . Shuddering at the thought, I tightened my grip on Viktor's hand. He squeezed back gently in return but didn't turn to look at me. He was just as vigilant as everyone else, watching our surroundings, listening for voices or footsteps, trying to gauge the energy in the air.

Or maybe that was just me.

Something was different, though. I wasn't really sure what it was until we turned the corner and started down Laburnum Avenue. I was plenty familiar with that part of town; I'd grown up only a few blocks away, though I hadn't been back in years. Things looked pretty much like I remembered, with the exception of a few abandoned cars parked against the curb, their windows smashed. There were actually fewer cars around than would be expected after an apocalypse. Then again, most adults had taken their cars with them when they'd left. Anything that had been left behind was the property of those who'd chosen (or been forced) to stay behind with a bunch of jacked-up, magic-wielding teenagers. Either that, or they were surplus, left behind by the car-wealthy older folks who'd chosen to take only one vehicle with them. Most of those vehicles were now nothing more than junk. In the first few months after the evacuation, there'd been some joyriding. Any electric cars had stopped working right away (probably disabled remotely), and had subsequently been trashed. The gas-powered vehicles that had survived the joyrides had eventually had the remaining fuel siphoned out of them, and then they'd met the same fate as the EVs. If this nightmare ever ended, there would be plenty of debris to clean up:

pebbles of broken glass, torn-up seats that had been removed and then abandoned, slashed and abandoned tires, burned-out hulls.

My hair started to bristle as we continued down the street toward the high school. I'd never gone there, of course, having been homeschooled my whole life. But I'd passed it plenty of times, and never had I felt what I was feeling as we trudged down the street, our shoes crunching on the remains of shattered car windows. Curiosity? Sure. Longing? A bit, especially when I'd happened to see people my own age gathered in friendly groups out on the big front lawn. No, what I felt now was something different. Something . . . otherworldly. That was the only way I could describe it.

I saw the fence before I saw the building itself. That had definitely not been there before. The yellow mesh panels stretched up over our heads. They must've been at least eight feet high. Curls of razor wire topped the fencing. For some reason, the sight made me shudder.

"That's the high school," Viktor whispered, his mouth so close to my ear that his breath felt like a hot wind. I jerked away and glared up at him.

"I know that," I mouthed. He came to a stop, squeezing my hand, and I had no choice but to stop as well. He leaned closer once more.

"At night, you can apparently see the glow through the windows."

I pulled away a little so I could peer at him. "The Rift," I mouthed.

He nodded and turned to point. I followed his finger toward the school. Click had stopped, too, and was staring at the building, his posture rigid. As I looked past him, I could see the entrance, the glass-panelled doors chained and padlocked shut. My gaze drifted up to the second floor where a row of windows stretched across the front façade. I couldn't see much, really, past the reflections. Besides, it was the middle of the day.

Niesha, realizing that we'd all stopped, stormed back to us. With an angry wave of her hand, she gestured down the street. I started walking again, pulling Viktor with me. But Click didn't move. Niesha had to go over and lay her hand on his arm. He startled a little, and she leaned close to whisper something in his ear. I couldn't hear anything from that far away, but whatever she'd said, it got him moving again, and the four of us continued down the street, paradoxically moving deeper into danger as well as closer to safety.

—

It had been years since I'd been to a checkpoint, and, even then, it had just been to gather supplies. I'd never been to *this* checkpoint, though, and I was surprised to see how heavily fortified it was. That made sense, really, if it was the only one equipped for comings and goings.

My hand had been in Viktor's for hours at that point, and while he might not have minded the slimy film that had built up between our palms, I kind of did. As we left the last of the buildings in Permanent Marc's territory behind and approached the gap in the wall before us, I pulled my hand out of his grasp and wiped it on my thigh.

"Yeah," he said, keeping his voice low. "You sweat a lot, don't you?"

Niesha whirled on him like a snake. "Shut up!" she hissed.

"We haven't seen anyone in hours. Besides"—he swept his arm out, indicating the relatively empty space around us—"we're kind of in no-man's land here."

She marched back to him and grabbed his ear, pulling him down so she could not-so-quietly whisper into it. "If Marc finds out someone used his checkpoint—"

"It's not *his* checkpoint."

"Might as well be. Keep your mouth shut until we actually get there."

He straightened up as soon as she let go of his ear, clamping his mouth shut with a popping noise. He slid his heels together and gave her a cheeky salute. She looked like she wanted to smack him, but she probably didn't want to chance making that much noise. So she just whirled around and stormed down the street. I glanced at Viktor, who angled his head toward me with a grin. I shook my head and followed Niesha.

The wall that had been hastily erected around Kenyonville in the days after the Rift had opened was kind of a mishmash of materials. In some places, it was just a chainlink fence. In others, it was more solid, with metal bars. In some spots, it was cobbled together with sheet metal, which was pretty damn ugly to look at, but probably got the job done better than anything else. The wall that stretched on either side of the checkpoint gate was solid, topped with razor wire. I wasn't sure how anyone would've climbed up the vertical surface, anyway, so the razor wire was probably redundant, more of a deterrent than anything else. The sliding gate stood open, as all the gates did. I wasn't sure why the checkpoints even had gates at all. Maybe the military figured they would need to close them at some point, leaving us all inside to . . . what? I wasn't sure. Start a Rifter war? It hadn't happened yet, but anything was possible.

"Let me do the talking," Niesha said, falling back to walk alongside us. Viktor snorted.

"You think they're not going to want to talk to the rest of us?"

She gave him a dark look. "We've got one shot at this, Viktor. If you mess it up, so help me—"

"How do you think I'm going to mess it up? I want to get out of here as much as you do."

"I doubt that."

"I'm not an idiot. I can handle a few questions."

"Yeah, I'm sure. That's all I want you to do, anyway. Don't offer any info they don't ask for. Just answer."

"Truthfully?"

"Yes, truthfully," she snapped, then clamped her mouth shut as if something had just occurred to her.

"We weren't tested," he said. "So maybe—"

She held up her hand to cut him off. "We both have families who left. So we probably are in the records, even if we didn't get tested." She frowned. "And you went with the aid orgs. There'll be a record of that."

"What about Léa?"

"What about me?" I asked.

Viktor shrugged. "You said you didn't have anyone out there. So I'm guessing your family didn't leave."

"So?"

"Were you tested for pinkhands?"

"No."

"So there won't be any record of you," Niesha said thoughtfully. "Beyond the usual."

"What's the usual?"

"Birth certificate. Medical records."

"Vet records," Viktor added with a snort.

"Shut up," I snapped.

Niesha shot us both a warning look. "Cool it. But . . . that's a good point. Maybe you *should* use a different name."

"Why?"

"Because if, for some reason, our names are flagged as Rifters, you might still be able to get out."

I gaped. "You think I'd go without you?"

"Better one of us than none of us."

"And what the hell do you think I'd do out there all by myself? You said you'd help me. Without that, I . . ." Frowning, I looked down at the pavement in front of me. *I'd have to do it all on my own,* I thought. Not that I hadn't done that before, albeit inside the Rift Zone. Viktor clamped a hand on my shoulder, causing me to startle.

"Forget it," he said, and I looked up to find him watching me with a concerned expression in his mismatched eyes. "We do this together, or we don't do it at all."

"So you'd condemn her to a life in the Rift Zone when she might be able to escape?" Niesha asked.

"You don't know she'd be able to escape. If they're going to find a reason to keep *us* in here, they'd find a reason to keep *her* in here. And the more lies we tell, the worse it could be if we're found out."

She grunted. "Weren't you the one who just asked if we were going to be truthful?"

"Yeah, but not because I was planning on lying. I was just wondering if you were."

"Jesus," she muttered. "I am *so* glad this is almost over."

"No, you're not. Come on, admit it. You're going to miss me when I'm gone, aren't you?"

"Can a person miss head lice?"

"Hmm . . . I prefer the comparison to herpes you used a few months ago."

"I wouldn't miss that, either."

He shrugged carelessly. Niesha's expression was light, though, as she shook her head, and I could see that, even though she liked to complain, she was going to miss their playful jabs.

CHAPTER 8

THE CHECKPOINT

I didn't see the guards until we'd almost reached the opening in the wall. And then, there they were in their fatigues, helmets strapped on tight, scary-looking guns in their hands. Those guns weren't pointed at us, but I suspected that could change at any moment.

"It's Friday!" one of the guards shouted. She walked toward the middle of the gate and planted her feet, both hands on her weapon.

"TGIF!" Viktor called out. Niesha stiffened, but she didn't say anything, either to him or to the guard.

"Distribution is on Saturdays at eleven-hundred hours. You'll have to come back tomorrow."

"We're not here for food," Niesha said. She held her hands out to the sides, perhaps trying to appear non-threatening. But it seemed to have the opposite effect. The guard raised her weapon. We all came to a quick stop. Even Click.

"Spit," Viktor whispered.

"Lower your hands to your sides!" the guard barked. "Palms on your thighs."

Niesha did as she was asked, slowly, as if she didn't want to make any sudden moves and spook the guard. When her hands were plastered to her sides, the guard jerked the muzzle of the gun at the rest of us.

"Everyone. Palms on your thighs."

My heart hammered in my chest. It was really happening. Ever since Niesha had told us about her plan, it had been a vague, hazy sort of notion. I'd imagined it, of course, but since I didn't really know what to expect, those daydreams had been sort of ephemeral. Now that it was happening, though, I wasn't sure if anything was going to go the way she'd hoped. My stomach felt sour, and I could hear the thud of my heart in my ears, drowning out almost everything else. I wanted to turn and run, back to the devil I knew, but I figured that would probably get me a bullet in the ass.

If I were lucky.

"We want to apply for exit," Niesha said, her voice unnecessarily loud. Maybe her heart was kicking up a fuss, too, and she couldn't hear that well.

The guard just stared at her for a moment, as if she couldn't believe what she was hearing. "Are you serious?"

"You think we'd risk coming down here and having guns pointed in our faces if we weren't?"

The woman with the gun jerked her head, and the guard who'd been lurking on the other side of the gate stepped into the open space. His gun was still pointed at the ground.

"Ages?" he asked.

"Seventeen through twenty-two," Niesha said.

"Then you're Rifters."

"No."

"The whole generation was affected."

"Yeah … at first, maybe. But something's changed." Niesha seemed to be struggling to steady her voice. I wasn't sure if that was because she was afraid or angry. "We don't have pinkhands anymore. You can test us if you like."

"We haven't done any testing in years. There's no point."

"Well, maybe you should start doing it again. Like I said, something's changed. And we shouldn't be stuck in here if we're no danger to anyone else. Right?"

He didn't say anything. My gaze moved to the other guard, who still had her gun pointed at Niesha.

"I have a contact on the outside," Niesha said, tilting her chin up just the tiniest bit. "Can you imagine what would happen if it was discovered that you were holding unaffected kids in here, keeping them separated from their parents?" She shook her head slowly. "Not a good look."

The male guard said something to his partner that I didn't catch. The woman slowly lowered her gun.

"Keep your hands on your thighs," she said, stepping back to the side of the gate. She reached for something just out of view, and then there was a sort of mumbling, followed by a crackle. I glanced at Viktor, but he was staring straight ahead, chewing on his lower lip.

Whatever the guard was doing, it seemed to take forever. It was probably just a few minutes, but when you were facing a couple of military personnel with some pretty scary weaponry, that time seemed a lot longer. I could hear my breath whistling, even over the sound of my heart pounding in my ears. It was a good thing Viktor had taught us his tricks, because I would've been flaring like a sparkler otherwise. I could feel the energy trickling down my body, under my clothes, and I was tempted to look down to see if I could detect any sort of glow through them. But I didn't dare.

At last, the female guard stepped back into view. She approached her partner and spoke low, keeping her head turned away from us so I couldn't even read her lips. A moment later, she turned and waved her hand, and her partner stepped aside.

"Come on, then. Hands on thighs. If I see so much as a spark of pink . . ."

"We're not *that* stupid," Viktor said.

"I'd say you're pretty damn stupid, coming here to apply for exit. This is a quarantine zone."

"Yeah . . . so why are you waving us in?"

"Because the higher-ups are curious. Personally, I don't see what's so interesting about a bunch of liars."

"Maybe they're bored," he said. He walked forward,

keeping his arms tightly against his sides, which made for an awkward sort of gait. "I mean, you guys've been sitting out here for over three years, making sure nothing gets in or out."

"You Rifters get plenty of food."

He snorted. "You think the average kid sees any of that?"

"Stop talking," Niesha hissed back at him. She was a few paces ahead. "Jesus. Do you know how to follow instructions, or is it pathological?"

"I'm following instructions now, aren't I?" He shrugged his shoulders a couple of times, as if to emphasize his hands glued to his thighs.

"Just shut up," she ground out through clenched teeth.

"Got a smartass here, do we?" the male guard asked, his eyebrows raised as we shuffled past him through the open gate.

"You could say that." Niesha kept her gaze straight ahead as she walked out of the Rift Zone. I almost expected to feel something when I stepped over that boundary, but I didn't. Really, why would I have? The border was just an arbitrary line. Kenyonville was kind of on its own, surrounded by nothing but fields, forests, and a handful of roads that led in and out of town ... all of which were now guarded by checkpoints.

The road ahead of us was pretty empty, though. On either side were a few portable buildings, like the kind used as offices on construction sites. Beyond one of those, on the left and tucked away from the road, was a large white tent.

"Supplies?" Viktor asked, tipping his chin toward the structure. The guards didn't answer him. "Oh, come on. You can tell me."

"No, they can't," Niesha said, her voice almost lost as she kept her head turned away from us. "You think they want every kid in town storming the place?"

"Everyone knows there are supplies out here. But who are we going to tell? We're getting out, remember?"

"Don't count your chickens," the male guard said with a glance back at us. His jaw twitched as he looked at Viktor. "Might want to get Frazier to have a look at that."

"At what?" Viktor asked.

"Your face."

He came to an abrupt stop. "There's something wrong with my face?" he asked, his eyes widening. Niesha stopped and looked back at us, shaking her head slowly.

"Knock it off."

He turned to me, and then to Click, before finally fixing his gaze on her. "What's wrong with my face? Is there something on it?" His voice rose a little in mock panic. "You guys would tell me, right?"

The guard snorted.

"Welcome to our world," Niesha muttered.

"Sounds fun." He gestured to one of the portables on the right. It was a little larger than the others, with bright white walls, two windows blocked with what looked like solid blinds, and a bristle of antennae on the roof. We walked up the steps in single file—Niesha first, followed by Click, then me, and Viktor in the rear—and through the door the female guard held open for us. As we stepped into the dimmer space, it took a few moments for my eyes to adjust. When they did, I let out a little squeak and edged close to Viktor. His hand slid into mine, and I didn't even care that it was slippery with sweat. The door closed with a click of finality, blocking out the sunshine.

"What is this?" Niesha asked, her words slow and clipped. A note of wary suspicion ran through them, as if she were trying to figure out the situation.

But I could already tell we had just walked straight into trouble.

CHAPTER 9

TESTING, TESTING . . .

The figure in pale green scrubs on the far side of the room looked up from her laptop. I only saw that out of the corner of my eye, though. The rest of my attention was drawn to the white examination table that sat in the middle of the space, surrounded by monitors and machines. There were two pieces that jutted out from the sides, like platforms for arms. Loose straps dangled from the ends.

I have to get out of here. I have to get out of here. But I couldn't move. I stayed plastered to Viktor's rigid side, pressed close enough that I could cling to his hand without anyone seeing. The guards and their guns had stayed outside, but that didn't mean I felt any safer in that room.

"You're here for testing?" the woman asked. I swallowed hard. My mouth felt like I'd been licking dust from the top of Grandpa's old TV. I didn't think I could answer if I tried.

"What is this?" Niesha asked again, so I knew she was seeing what I was seeing. What we were all seeing.

"What does it look like?" The woman—Dr. Frazier, based on the name tag on her scrubs—frowned. She was older, probably in her forties, with artificially blond hair and striking blue eyes. She gave off sort of a mom vibe, but that might've just been because she reminded me a bit of Grandma, who was the only mother I'd ever known. "You wanted to be tested, right?"

"Depends," Viktor said. His voice, usually so sure and steady, held an edge of wobbliness that I'd never heard before. I tightened my grip on his hand. "What's with the mad scientist's table?"

The doctor glanced over at the object in question. "A precaution. For your protection as well as ours."

"Not necessary. We don't have pinkhands anymore. See?" He lifted his free hand from his thigh, made his little fart noise, and jerked toward her with a non-glowing hand. She flinched, just as my panic flared, and I was super grateful those guards had waited outside.

"Impressive," she said. "But I'm afraid I can't take your word for it."

"Of course not," Niesha said. "Which is why we came to be tested. But I thought . . ."

The doctor shook her head and walked over to a locked cabinet at the side of the room. She pulled out a large glass vial, as well as four huge syringes. I squeaked a little and took a step back.

"It looks worse than it is," she said, heading for the scary table and depositing the instruments of torture on the little metal cart beside it, which was already loaded with supplies: alcohol wipes, cotton swabs, a couple of rubber tourniquets, and a few other things I couldn't identify. "Who wants to go first?"

"What do you mean?" Niesha asked, casting a worried glance at the rest of us. "I thought . . . Don't you just try to startle us?"

Dr. Frazier smiled. It was a nice smile, but I couldn't really appreciate it at that moment, what with my heart flopping around in my chest. "That's how we used to do things. But it's hard on the ears. And potentially traumatic." She rested a hand on the table. "Not everybody reacts the same way to being startled, either. This way, we can control for variables better."

"This way?"

"Just a shot of epi. It's unpleasant, but we'll get our answers fast."

Oh, shit. Learning to channel the Rift energy downward was one thing, especially when a lot of it had to do with my emotions. But this—trying to channel Rift energy while lying down, after having the response chemically induced—was another. I looked at Niesha in desperation, hoping to catch her gaze and let her know we needed to abandon the plan.

We were probably all going to be found out. Even if the rest of them somehow managed to do it, I knew I wasn't going to be able to. I'd just barely gotten a handle on the process. And now . . .

"Why epi?" Niesha asked, then shook her head. "I mean, I know pinkhands can be triggered by strong emotions. Does the epi activate the virus or something?" I was pretty sure she didn't want to know the answer, either. She was stalling, maybe trying to figure out a plan B. But I already knew what that was: Get the hell out of there.

The doctor shook her head. "We've learned a few things about Rifters in the last three years. Much of it is still a mystery, but we do know that it's not viral."

"Really?" Viktor asked, sounding almost disappointed. "So we can't rampage through the countryside and spread it to the unsuspecting villagers?"

She raised her eyebrows. "Would you want to?"

"No. Just asking."

With another shake of her head, she smiled. "The cause is likely a combination of things . . . none of which are catching. First, age."

"Well, we know *that*," Niesha said.

"Maybe I should clarify. It's not so much the age as what happens at that age."

"Hormones," Viktor said, nodding sagely. "Well, we do have plenty."

"I'm sure you do. So far, we've been able to determine that it's a combination of hormones, a certain stage of brain development, and proximity to the Rift. Which is why only people of a certain age in this town were affected. *Are* affected," she corrected herself. Her voice dipped low, and, for a moment, I thought I caught a hint of tightness. But she pushed a smile onto her face and went on. "As far as we can tell, nobody grows out of the glowing hands, either."

"How would you know that?" Niesha asked.

"Do you think you're the first ones to apply for exit?"

Viktor shifted at my side. His hand felt uncomfortably hot, and I wanted to pull away. But I didn't. "How many people have passed the test?" he asked.

"You'd be the first."

"*Cool!*"

"You think you're going to pass?"

"I *know* we're going to pass," he said, the familiar cockiness back in his voice. He pulled his hand out of mine (it was so moist that I actually heard it) and strode over to the table. "So, where do you want me?"

Niesha and I exchanged a glance. "Maybe I should go first," she said, turning back to the doctor. Viktor opened his mouth to protest, but Niesha struck him with such a venomous glare that he clamped his mouth shut with a pop.

"Okay. Age before beauty." He swept his hand to the side, inviting her onto the table. Dr. Frazier shook her head, then went over to her desk and leaned over the laptop.

"Name?"

"Niesha Thomason."

The doctor tapped on the keyboard. "I've got a Williams Thomason."

"Yeah. That's my dad."

"Evacuated?"

"Mm-hmm."

The doctor glanced up. "Why am I not finding any record of you?"

"There should be one. I had to register to stay in our house while Mom and Dad got the hell out."

"I wouldn't be surprised if some records got lost along the way. That week before the evacuation was barely organized chaos."

"I remember." Niesha looked down at the table, then over at Dr. Frazier. "Some little shits just burned down our house, and I'm really tired of this place, so . . ."

"I think we're all tired of it," the doctor said. "But that doesn't mean I can let you just walk out of here."

"We know. That's why we came to get tested." With a sigh, Niesha hoisted herself onto the table and lay down, arranging her arms on the smaller platforms. The sight sent a shiver of ice through my body.

Dr. Frazier tapped at the keyboard once more, then straightened up. But before she could say anything, a beeping noise filled the room. She frowned, glanced at the screen, and hurried toward the doorway on the far side of the space. It was covered in foggy curtains of plastic, so I couldn't see anything beyond, although I suspected it was probably another connected porta-ble. As soon as she was out of earshot (or so I hoped), I rushed closer to the table.

"I need to go," I whispered. "Now. I won't be able to do this."

"Sure, you will," Viktor said. The ease in his tone made me want to slap him.

"I've just barely learned not to fry you when you piss me off," I hissed. "And that's when I'm in control. You think I'm going to have any control over my hands when she injects that stuff?"

"If you can't do it," Niesha said, staring up at the ceiling, "chances are that none of us will be able to. But we're here, so we might as well give it a shot."

My gaze drifted to the vial. "As long as that's what she says it is. What if this is some sort of trap?"

She snorted. "What kind of trap?"

"Maybe they want to study Rifters." I jabbed a hand at the plastic sheeting. Despite the fact that my heart was racing so hard I felt like I was going to pass out, my hands weren't flaring. I could feel the Rift energy, though, just below the surface, ready to burst through if I gave it the slightest opportunity. "What do you think she's got in that other room? They could be vivi-secting kids. She said it had to do with brain development. What if they're actually . . ."

"Prying out their brains?" Viktor suggested. "You think these people are that evil?"

"Maybe not intentionally. Maybe they think they're

doing good by studying kids like us. If they can figure out how Rifters work, they'd be heroes. Or, at least, they'd think they are."

"They did abandon a whole generation inside a quarantine zone," Niesha said slowly. She sat up, frowning. "But do you really think she would—"

"Sorry about that," the doctor said, pushing past the plastic. She pulled off a pair of gloves and tossed them into a biohazard bin beside the doorway before striding toward us. Viktor, Click, and I all moved back, leaving Niesha alone on the table.

"What's in there?" Viktor asked. I turned to him in disbelief, but since his ruined eye was the one closest to me, he didn't notice. "You dissecting Rifters?"

"Viktor!" Niesha hissed. She shook her head. "Ignore him. He's just—"

"It's fine. I'd be suspicious, too. After what you must've gone through in the Zone . . ." Her smile was sad as she reached into the cart and pulled a new pair of gloves from a box. "No, no dissection. No vivisection, either," she said with a quick glance in my direction. I felt myself blanch.

She got Niesha to lie back as she readied one of the syringes. Then she fastened the straps around Niesha's wrists, trapping her on the table. My head was shaking in little tiny jerks, as if my body were saying "no, no, no" all on its own.

"This is not going to be comfortable, all right? I need to get at your thigh. Can I pull your pants down a few inches?" When Niesha nodded, the doctor unfastened her pants and tugged them down, exposing her thighs, one of which she swabbed with alcohol. "You ready?" she asked, picking up the needle and plunging out the last bit of air.

"I guess," Niesha said. Her hands tightened into fists.

I was too horrified to do anything other than wince as the doctor stabbed the needle deep into Niesha's thigh muscle.

"So," Viktor said a few seconds later when the doctor had discarded the needle in a bright yellow box. "How do you feel?"

Niesha took a deep breath and let it out slowly. "Like I just came face to face with a grizzly bear in my backyard." She blew out another breath. "Whew. How long is this going to last?"

"The worst of it'll be over in a few minutes," Dr. Frazier said. "You might feel a bit weird for a few hours, but that'll pass." She looked down at Niesha's hands with a frown. They were still in tight fists, but there was no visible glow. "Interesting. Relax your hands, please."

Niesha complied, slowly. I held my breath. But nothing happened. She pressed her fingertips against the padded surfaces under them.

"You're looking a bit . . . sparkly," Viktor said. The doctor laughed.

"Increased perspiration." She unfastened the restraints and discarded that pair of gloves. "You'll be sweating in a minute, too."

"Ooh. Fun."

I glanced up at him, marvelling at how he could keep up that cheeky lightness, even in our current situation. He was watching Niesha, who sat up slowly. She did look a little moist, especially around her temples.

"Who's next?" Dr. Frazier asked. Viktor took a step forward, but Click wiggled ahead of him and hopped up on the table as soon as Niesha had stumbled away. "Might be easier if you pull your pants down first. And make sure that skirt is out of the way."

Click did as she said, yanking his jeans down to his ankles before jumping back on the table. Viktor snorted.

"I wouldn't be so eager," he warned him. "That's not liquid fairy dust."

"Is that some sort of new drug in the Zone?" Dr. Frazier asked, eyebrows raised as she headed back to her laptop.

"No," Niesha said. She sounded a bit breathless. "That's just a smartass trying to be clever." She blinked hard a few times and pressed her fingers to the side of her neck, checking her pulse. "Is this dangerous?"

"Not in the dose I gave you. It's uncomfortable, but you should be fine." Tapping on the keyboard, she shook her head. "Name?"

"Ah-ee," Click said, punctuating his name with that little noise from the back of his throat. The doctor looked up.

"Could you spell that?"

"Your guess is as good as ours," Viktor said.

"A-I with a dieresis," Niesha said, her voice absent. Viktor turned to her in surprise.

"Diarrhea?"

"Dieresis. Two little dots above the— Never mind." She blew out a breath and shook her hands in front of her as she stepped in place.

"Having fun?"

"Remind me to ask you the same thing when it's your turn."

Dr. Frazier was busy frowning at her laptop. "Last name?"

"No idea," Niesha said.

"He's an exchange student," Viktor added.

"From where?"

"Heck if we know." He shrugged. "Some place called Reefa."

"Reefa?" the doctor repeated. "Tenerife, maybe?"

"Is that west of here?"

"No." She thought for a moment. "The Great Barrier Reef? Maybe he's from Australia."

"I think his English would be better," Viktor mused, looking over at his friend who was lying on the table, jeans around his ankles, skirt pulled up around his waist. "Whoa, Click! None of us want to see that." Click lifted his head, looked down, and quickly tugged the hem of his skirt a little lower. The doctor laughed.

"Well, it doesn't really matter. I'm not seeing anything

here for an Aï at all. We'll just use Doe." She tapped on the keys again before abandoning the laptop. As she pulled on a new pair of gloves, she looked down at the boy on the table. "Does he understand what I'm going to do?"

"Probably," Niesha said. "He seems to understand English pretty well, even if he doesn't speak it."

We watched as the doctor restrained his arms, then pulled his skirt up just a little bit more, an amused expression on her face. When she plunged the needle into his thigh, he sucked in a gasp.

Predictably, nothing happened, so she released him. He pulled his jeans back up and fastened them, a strange grin on his face.

"Um . . . you seemed to enjoy that way too much," Viktor said, to which he got a double thumbs up. Dr. Frazier laughed.

"Next," she said. Viktor strode over to the table and arranged his long limbs on it. I expected Dr. Frazier to go back to her laptop, but, instead, she bent over Viktor's face, gently turning his head so she could have a better look. "What happened here?"

"Why does everybody keep asking that? Is there something wrong with my face?"

Niesha sighed with a shake of her head. "He fried himself."

"Doing what?"

"Shaving."

"Really." The doctor's bemused tone matched the expression on her face.

"The facial hair is coming," Viktor said. "I'm just a late bloomer."

"How old are you?"

"Seventeen."

She peered closer, peeling his eyelids apart so she could see his cloudy eye. "You've got a few years of maturing to go. But don't get your hopes up. I doubt you'll ever have a full beard."

"Dang."

"How much can you see?"

"Light. A bit of colour." He shrugged as she finally let go of his face. "It's fine."

She grunted. "It's far from *fine*. But those injuries are beyond anything I can help you with here. You'd need a plastic surgeon, for starters."

"Who says I want to fix anything? Ladies *love* the scar." He lifted his head and gave me a cheeky grin. I quickly looked away as I felt my cheeks warm.

Dr. Frazier headed over to her laptop. "Name?"

"Viktor Knowles."

"Right." She tapped it in. "Marlena and Craig Goodman?"

"My aunt and uncle."

She frowned. "You have a cousin on the outside?"

"Her name's in there, but Niesha's isn't?" He peered in her direction. "Wow. No offence, Doc, but that's not the sort of organization I expect from the military."

The doctor's lips twitched. "How old is your cousin?"

"Thirteen now, I guess." He let his head fall back on the table. "Good thing she was a late bloomer like me, or she would've gotten stuck here, too."

Dr. Frazier didn't say anything to that, but just finished typing something before returning to the table and strapping him down. She grabbed another pair of gloves and readied the next syringe. My heart was racing so hard already that I felt like I was going to pass out. Seeing Niesha and Click pass the tests hadn't really helped; if anything, it made me more nervous because I'd pretty much convinced myself that I was going to fail and let everyone down. I glanced at my hands, expecting to see them glowing a bright, juicy pink. But they just looked like a regular pair of hands.

"Ready?" the doctor asked, and I looked back over at Viktor.

"Give it to me," he said. "I can take— Ow! You could've warned me."

"I did."

He said nothing for a moment. I watched his hands, but of course they stayed unlit. Dr. Frazier watched, too, wonder on her face.

"Interesting. I don't know what's changed, but I haven't seen anything like this in three—"

"Woo!" Viktor hooted, causing all of us to jump. "Now that's what I call a rush!"

The doctor laughed. "Enjoyed that, did you?"

"I've had better."

"Viktor!" Niesha hissed, but Dr. Frazier just shook her head in amusement and reached to unbuckle the restraints. As soon as he was free, Viktor sat up like a shot, rubbing his wrists like he'd had handcuffs on them for hours.

"What? Haven't you?" he asked, sliding to the floor and striding over to me. A little noise, almost a yelp, escaped me as he reached for my hand. "Come on, Léa. Your turn."

I wrenched away, glaring at him. "Don't touch me."

He raised his eyebrows. "Just trying to help."

"Well, don't. I can walk over there just fine." But my feet stayed where they were, rooted to the floor. I looked at Click, bouncing on the balls of his feet, still jacked up from the look of it. I turned to Niesha, who gave me an encouraging nod.

What do I do? I thought, my inner voice almost a wail. *They're almost free. I'm going to screw this up for them, and they'll hate me. They'll pretend it's fine, but I'll know it's not. And we'll have to go back into the Rift Zone, and I'll still have to live with them, and everything will be so awkward.*

"Needle phobia?" the doctor asked. I turned to her. Her expression was soft. Not judging at all. "It helps if you don't look."

I shook my head. "Yeah. Okay." Rubbing my wet palms on my thighs, I stepped toward the table, feeling like I was heading for my doom. Needles weren't the problem. Letting down the only three people I had left in the world was.

"It's actually kind of cool," Viktor said. "You'll see."

I didn't even feel like shooting him a dirty look. I undid my jeans, yanked them down to my knees (glad my underwear was still decent and not full of holes), and hoisted myself onto the table. Dr. Frazier took the opportunity to fasten the restraints.

"Don't you need my name?" I squeaked out. She nodded.

"Right. Sorry." She checked the restraint on my right wrist again before heading over to her laptop.

I lifted my head and tried to send Niesha an SOS with my gaze. Something was not right. I wasn't sure what, but . . . I could feel it.

"Name?" the doctor asked.

"Léa Young."

She typed it in, and her frown deepened. "Another exchange student?"

"No. I've lived in Kenyonville all my life."

She shook her head. "I'm not seeing anything here. Do your parents have the same last name as you?"

"My father does."

"And where is he? Did he not evacuate?"

I chewed on my lip for a moment before answering. "My grandparents raised me. I never even met my father. My mom put his name on my birth certificate, but . . ."

"Where's your mother?"

"No idea. Not in the Rift Zone." I swallowed hard. I could feel Niesha and Viktor staring.

"So you lived with your grandparents?"

"My grandmother died before the Rift."

"And your grandfather?" she prompted. I closed my eyes, even though doing that when I thought about Grandpa often caused a sort of movie to play behind my eyelids. And *that* was not the sort of movie I wanted to watch at that moment.

"Gone," I said. "I don't have anyone in the Zone, okay?"

"Okay." The doctor's voice was soft. There was another tap of fingers on keys, and then footsteps. I opened my eyes to find her standing beside me, pulling on yet another pair of gloves. The pungent tang of alcohol zinged into my nose as she swabbed my thigh, making me feel like I was about to sneeze. She readied the last syringe, and I watched a tiny bit of the liquid squirt from the end of the needle. "I want you to look away, all right? Close your eyes if it helps."

The alcohol swab had felt cold. But that was nothing compared to the heat that soared through me when the epi went to work. I sucked in a gasp as my heart rate skyrocketed. My whole body felt like it was vibrating. And then . . . I felt it. The warm, prickling sensation of Rift energy as it surged down my arms. In a panic, I tried to pull it back, direct it toward my feet. But it wasn't so easy when I was lying down. I let out a squeal that was part terror, part disappointment, and a few parts shame. *I'm going to ruin everything!*

"Hey, Doc," Viktor said, his voice way louder than it needed to be in such a small space, "I'm not feeling so—" He broke off, and the next thing I heard (and felt) was a mighty *whump* as a heavy weight hit the floor. I opened my eyes to see Dr. Frazier hurrying away from my side. Viktor was sprawled out on the floor, eyes closed, completely still. I tried to sit up but was thwarted by the restraints. Out of the corner of my eye, I saw pink.

My hands were flaring.

"What did you give us?" I shouted, my voice so loud it almost hurt my ears. Niesha jerked her head toward me, and in her gaze was a warning. I frowned in confusion. She twitched her fingers, as if shaking off Rift energy, and raised her eyebrows at me.

"Just epinephrine," Dr. Frazier said, kneeling at Viktor's side. She gave his cheek a gentle pat. "Hey. Viktor. Can you hear me?"

There was a little grunt. And then, "Mom?"

"No, I'm not your mom." She sat back on her heels. "You okay?"

He opened his eyes slowly, his eyelids fluttering. "Am I dead?"

"Hardly. You just fainted."

"Oh." He lifted one hand and pressed it against his forehead. "I guess I can't hold my epi."

She laughed. "Looks like it." She grabbed his arm and helped him sit up. As relief flooded through me, I remembered my hands. I flicked my fingers hard, dislodging as much of the energy as I could while trying to push the rest down toward my toes. As the pinkhands cooled, my fingers returned to their normal colour. And not a moment too soon, because Dr. Frazier chose that moment to glance at me.

"You feeling okay?" she asked. I nodded. After she helped Viktor back to his feet, she came over and unfastened the restraints. I got down off that table so fast that I almost forgot about my jeans and nearly tripped in my haste to get away.

"So . . . can we go?" Niesha asked as the doctor went back to her laptop and began to type furiously. I looked up at Viktor, who was standing there, rubbing his shoulder. When he noticed me looking, he glanced down with a quick smile . . . and a wink. I gaped at him, but of course I couldn't do more than that with Dr. Frazier still in the room with us.

"The rules are that nobody can leave the Rift Zone unless they pass the test."

"Yeah . . . and we all passed. So what's the problem?"

Dr. Frazier looked up. And then she looked at me.

CHAPTER 10

THE BOY IN THE BED

"She passed!" Viktor cried. "Her hands didn't flare at all."

Dr. Frazier raised an eyebrow. "And you saw all this while passed out?"

He clamped his lips together. But then he clenched his fists.

"Viktor," Niesha began, because she could probably see as well as I could that he was right on the edge. I had no idea why . . . although maybe the epi had something to do with it.

"I'd like to remind you," Dr. Frazier said slowly, as if she were talking to a wild animal, "that the guards are right outside. So if you get any ideas about using those hands to—"

"We don't have farting pinkhands!" Viktor shouted. I backed away from him, alarmed by the intensity and volume.

"Keep your voice down, please." She fixed him with a warning look. "If they come in here, my hands are tied."

"What are you talking about?" Niesha asked. "You're getting ready to send us back into the Rift Zone, which is presumably what those guards want, too."

The doctor didn't say anything. She looked at Viktor, who was trembling beside me, his fists in tight balls. Somehow, he still had the Rift energy under control. She looked at Click, who wore a confused expression. The bouncing had slowed, but it hadn't stopped; that antsiness needed an outlet. She looked at Niesha, whose expression was a mix of confusion, betrayal, and disappointment. And then she looked at me, the person who'd just dashed the hopes of four people because she couldn't manage to keep herself together for a few seconds.

"You're still a Rifter," she said quietly. My mouth opened, all on its own, as if it wanted to hurl a denial right back at her. But it couldn't. She sighed. "I don't know how the rest of you did it. I could run some tests—"

"No," Viktor said, his voice low. "No more tests."

"We did what you asked," Niesha said.

"And I failed." They all looked at me. I pulled my hands into tight fists and stared at the floor. Nobody said anything, though I was willing them to with all my might. I needed someone to tell me it was okay (even though it wasn't), that we'd think of something else (even though this had been our best idea), that we'd all just go home and things would be like they were before (even though I knew that wasn't possible). My heart was still racing, and my mouth felt dry. I looked up and took a step back. "You guys go ahead. It's fine. We knew this might happen."

Niesha shook her head. "We stick together."

"I'm not going to be the reason you're stuck here! It's one thing fucking up my own life. I don't want to be responsible for fucking up three more."

The doctor watched me for a few moments. Her expression was hard to read. At last, she walked over to the plastic curtains, beckoning with one hand. "There's something you need to see."

Viktor snorted. "Like heck we're going to step in there. What's the plastic for? To keep the walls clean from blood spatter?"

She stopped, looking stung. "Do you really think so little of me?"

"You're on the outside," Niesha said. "You'll find that a lot of us have trust issues with the people who left us in the Rift Zone."

The doctor's expression turned so sad that I wondered if she were about to cry. Through some sort of sheer will, though, she didn't. She just nodded. "I know. So you need to see this. Maybe you'll understand."

"Understand what?" Niesha asked, but the doctor didn't answer. Instead, she pulled back the curtain and gestured to us. Viktor and Niesha exchanged a look, while Click crept closer. When the other two decided to follow, I really had no choice but to do the same if I didn't want to be left all by myself.

The room past the plastic looked much the same as the one we'd been in: sleek, white, and sterile. But instead of the table with its restraints, it held something else. Something way worse than a needle and a stupid test.

"Oh, my god," Niesha breathed as her gaze fell on the white-swathed figure. It was obviously a person, though I couldn't determine the age or sex. The space around the bed was enclosed in walls of clear plastic that stretched all the way to the ceiling. Machines flashed and hummed, connected by tubes and wires to the poor person lying as still as death.

"What happened?" Viktor asked. "Is that … a Rifter?"

"His name is Carrick." The doctor gazed at the figure, a lost look in her eyes. But when Click stepped toward the bed, she snapped out of it fast, grabbing him by the arm. "Stay back. Nobody goes in there without gowning up."

"I thought you said there was no virus," Niesha said.

"There isn't. Distance isn't to protect you. It's to protect him."

"From what?"

"Bacteria. Fungi. Whatever you might be carrying on your bodies." She turned to us, her gaze solemn. "Third-degree burns over ninety percent of the body leave plenty of avenues for infection to get in."

I turned back to the person in the bed and stared, horrified.

"Burns from what?" Viktor asked. "Pinkballs?"

"What?"

"Riftballs," Niesha corrected. "Rift energy. Somebody did this to him?"

The doctor shook her head. "He did it to himself."

The room was silent. I didn't know what to say. Niesha and Viktor obviously didn't, either. Click kept staring, a look of desperation on his face. He pried at the doctor's fingers, and she finally let go.

"We failed you," Dr. Frazier said at last, turning to look at each of us in turn. "When we left. We were scared. We thought we were doing what was best. We thought the condition could spread. We didn't know what we do now. If I could go back and do things differently . . ."

"What?" Niesha asked. "What could you have done? Turned a bunch of Rifters loose outside the wall?"

"No. But maybe more of us could've stayed. Given the kids some hope." She looked over at Carrick. "He couldn't take it anymore."

"What happened?"

"He walked up to the gate and begged to be let out. When the guards refused to let him pass . . ." She swallowed hard. The look in her eyes had gone distant again. "He took off all his clothes. Then he rubbed that pink energy all over his body. Anywhere he could reach. By the time I heard the screaming . . ."

"Jesus," Niesha whispered.

"I failed him once," the doctor said quietly. "I'm not going to fail him again."

"Shouldn't he be in a proper hospital?" Viktor asked.

"He has everything he needs."

"Yeah, but—"

"He's your kid, isn't he?" Niesha asked. The room went silent. I swivelled my gaze to look at the doctor. She was staring at Carrick, her eyes bright. "I'm sorry," Niesha said.

"I abandoned him in there for three years. I'm not going to abandon him somewhere else. Not now. Whatever time he has left, he's going to spend it here, with me. And I can only hope that he feels it somehow." She closed her eyes as she took in a deep breath and let it out slowly. "I'm not going to fail anyone else," she said, opening her eyes and looking straight at me. "You passed."

"N-no, I didn't," I stammered.

"Yes, you did. I didn't see your hands flare. In fact, I haven't seen so much as a whiff of pink the whole time you four have been in here. So I'm signing off on your exit passes."

"But—" I began, just as Viktor grabbed me and pulled me into a hug, muffling my mouth against his chest.

"Great!" he said, his voice way too bright for the situation. I could feel his heart thumping wildly in his chest. "Awesome. Thanks, Doc. We really appreciate it."

"Not a problem," she said, stepping back into the

testing room. We followed, Viktor still sort of hugging my head. I flailed out of his grasp, giving him a dirty look. "There's no reason for you to be in the Zone," the doctor went on. "You're not Rifters anymore."

I just stood there in disbelief as she went to her laptop and tapped at the keys. Within minutes, we were each holding a printed copy of an exit pass.

"Show those to the guards on your way out. And don't let anything happen to those codes," she said, referring to the QR codes that were tucked in the bottom right corner of each form. "That's your proof."

"Of what?" Viktor asked. "That we're not crawling with Rift cooties?"

"It's not a virus," Niesha reminded him.

The doctor smiled, but it was a tired sort of expression. "You better get going. It's a long walk to the highway, and you'll want to get there before dark. The last bus to Goldvale passes through at seven."

"Thank you," Niesha said, the gratitude dripping from her words. "Really."

Dr. Frazier nodded. "Make the most of it, all right? Go live your lives and try to put the Zone behind you."

"We will," Viktor promised. He folded his pass in half and used it to give the doctor a salute. "Thanks, Doc."

"You're welcome."

As we stepped outside into the bright afternoon, the world felt different somehow. Lighter . . . and yet heavier at the same time. I couldn't shake the image of poor Carrick lying in that bed.

"Are burns to ninety percent of the body surviv-able?" I asked Niesha after we'd left the last of the guards behind and were trudging down the potholed road, Viktor and Click bringing up the rear. She shook her head.

"I don't think so. Poor kid."

"Kid?"

"Yeah. Dr. Frazier didn't look old enough to have a child my age. Carrick was probably just heading into puberty when the Rift happened."

"So he's . . . what? Thirteen? Fourteen?"

"Maybe." She shook her head. "He must've been absolutely desperate. To do that to yourself . . ."

She didn't have to finish the thought. I could barely fathom it myself. I looked back at Viktor, who gave me a quick smile. I whipped my head around to face for-ward again. But I was too late. A moment later, I heard footsteps on my right as he jogged to catch up.

"So," he said, "how'd I do?"

Niesha snorted. "Too hammy."

He gasped. "How dare you?"

"What are you talking about?" I asked. He elbowed me gently in the side.

"My performance back there. 'I can't hold my epi! Oh, woe is me!'" He clutched his chest and staggered. I turned to Niesha in disbelief. She just smirked.

"You knew?" I asked.

"I could tell," she corrected me. "It wasn't planned."

"Sure it was," Viktor said, straightening his gait. "I

just didn't share the plan with you. Luckily, you picked up on what I was doing."

"And what was that?" I asked, because I still wasn't really sure what they were talking about. Viktor shrugged.

"I thought you might freak out a little. So I wanted to be ready with a distraction, just in case."

"Just in case my hands flared and I ruined everything," I said miserably. He shook his head and threw his arm around my shoulders, pulling me close. I frowned, but I didn't try to get away.

"You didn't ruin anything," he said.

"I could have."

"But you didn't," Niesha said. "And, as it turned out, that whole charade was kind of unnecessary."

"It was kind of fun," Viktor said.

"Well, let's hope we don't have to have any more of that kind of fun." Staring down the road in front of us, she lifted her chin. "In a few hours . . ."

"Family," Viktor said. "People telling us what to do. Yay."

"If you're going to give your poor aunt and uncle as much grief as you give me, they might toss you back into the Rift Zone."

He just laughed and gave my shoulders a squeeze before pulling away. Given our height difference, it was easier to walk apart. But I still felt a strange sense of disappointment as his warmth left my side.

Get a grip, Léa. What the hell is wrong with you?

CHAPTER 11

TO GET WHERE WE'RE GOING

None of us had any money, so, once we got to the highway, we ended up hitching a ride in the back of some guy's pickup truck. Before the Rift, I never would've dreamed of hitchhiking. Way too dangerous, especially for a girl by herself. But there were four of us, and three-quarters of us were—unbeknownst to the driver—Rifters with built-in weaponry, so I figured we were probably safe enough. We lay down, shoulder to shoulder, in the bed of the truck, just so we wouldn't attract any attention, and watched the afternoon sky change colour as it drifted toward sunset.

The ride to Goldvale usually took about half an hour, but it seemed like a lot longer. The driver dropped us off near the bus station on the edge of town, and we clambered out of the truck, feeling a little bruised. At least, I did. The bed of a truck wasn't exactly a comfortable place to ride.

"So," Viktor said, stretching his arms above his head to work out the kinks, "what now?"

Niesha raised an eyebrow. "What do you think?"

"I *think*," he said, giving her a puzzled look, "that we can't be in two places at once. So where do we go first? Your place or mine?"

"Mine," she said quickly.

"You sure?"

"Yes, I'm sure. This whole thing was my idea, after all."

He shrugged. "Fine by me."

"You don't have to come with me, you know. We're out now. We can go our separate ways."

He widened his eyes as he mimed stabbing himself in the heart. "Are you breaking up with me?"

"Give me a break, Viktor. We'll see each other plenty, I'm sure. Goldvale isn't that big."

With a sigh, he looked up at the darkening sky. The clouds in the west were tinted orange, but the sky overhead was a deep blue. "I was kind of hoping to meet your parents."

"I would've thought you'd want to see your family ASAP."

"Oh, I want to see them. I'm just not sure they'll be ready to see me." He gestured to the scarred side of his face. "Aunt Marlena's not going to be happy. What am I supposed to tell her?"

"How about the truth?"

"The truth's too stupid."

She snorted. "Come up with a lie, then."

"She'd know it was a lie." He reached back and tightened his ponytail. "Can't we just come with you? One last evening together. And then Click and I will head out. Sound good?"

No, I thought before catching myself. The assumption was apparently that I would be staying with Niesha. But the thought of that just felt so weird. It had been the four of us for . . . well, not that long, really. And that was weird, too, because it felt like I'd known these people forever.

Niesha shrugged. "Suit yourself. I know Mom and Dad won't mind meeting my friends."

"Excellent." He rubbed his hands together and turned to look down the street. Goldvale was small, so it had much the same vibe as Kenyonville. At least, it had the same vibe as pre-Rift Kenyonville: quaint shopping plazas, landscaped boulevards, colourful banners on the lampposts. In Goldvale, though, everything looked a lot cleaner and more cared for. Kenyonville had that "the-apocalypse-happened-and-time-stopped" vibe that seemed to be missing in Goldvale. "Where do they live?" He turned to her with a worried expression. "Please tell me you have an address."

She gave him a dirty look. "Of course. I got it when I talked to them on the phone." Shaking her head, she started to walk. We fell into step beside her.

The sidewalks weren't wide enough for the four of us, though, so we split into two groups of two. Niesha and Viktor walked ahead of us, bantering and occasionally bickering. I had a feeling they were going to miss that, so they were getting in as much as they could before we all parted ways. I walked a few steps behind with Click. When I managed to catch his gaze, he gave me a weak smile.

"You okay?" I asked, because he looked a little off. Maybe it was just the deepening gloaming, but his skin looked more sallow than golden. He gave me a thumbs up.

"Are *you* okay?" Viktor asked. I turned to see him walking backward, staring at me with a concerned expression.

"Yeah. Why?"

"Well, I'm about to disappear from your life. That would make anyone miserable."

Niesha whacked him on the arm. "She'll be fine. In fact, she might not even want to stay in Goldvale, since she'd have to see *you* around all the time."

"Yeah. I guess." He blinked at me, his mismatched eyes looking strange in the shadows from the streetlights that had just flickered on overhead. "You going to go back to school?"

"Hard to go back when I've never been."

"You might like it."

"I'm too old."

He shook his head, still walking backward. "They might let you in. Extenuating circumstances and all that."

"Are *you* going back?"

"I might." His expression brightened. "We could be one of those high school power couples!"

Niesha chuckled. "Yeah, right."

"No, I'm serious. We'd be totally famous. We're from the Rift Zone, right? We'd be this mysterious curiosity. And I have the Scar of Intrigue."

"More like the Scar of Idiocy," I muttered.

"It'll be great," he said, ignoring my commentary. "Everybody would want to be our friend."

"I'm starting to think you've never been to high school at all," Niesha said, then fell silent for a moment. "Wait a minute. You're seventeen?"

"Yeah. Since February."

"And the Rift was three years ago."

"Yeah . . ." he said, not sure what she was getting at.

"It happened in March. So you were fourteen. The math doesn't work."

He shrugged. "I was a year ahead. I skipped Grade Two."

She gaped at him.

"What? I'm super smart."

For some reason, that made me giggle. I tried to clamp down on it, but not before he'd already noticed. He turned to me, a playful smile dancing on his undamaged features.

"Don't define my intelligence by one mistake. Besides, that was a startle reflex more than stupidity."

"You were trying to shave non-existent facial hair," Niesha pointed out.

"I wasn't *trying*. I was doing."

She snorted.

"Are you mocking my hairlessness?"

"No. Just your optimism. But," she said, holding up a hand as she saw he was about to retort, "look on the bright side. Trying to shave thick hair around that scar would be a bitch. You're probably better off being a baby-faced doofus."

He gasped dramatically, just as the heel of his boot caught a crack in the sidewalk. He stumbled but managed to catch himself before he could land on his ass.

"Turn around and walk properly," Niesha said, grabbing his arm and spinning him around.

"Yes, *Mom*," he said, his voice half sulk and all cheek.

——

By the time we reached Niesha's parents' place, it was dark. The suburban neighbourhood was quiet, but it wasn't the same sort of quiet as in Kenyonville. This was a lot more . . . friendly. For one thing, we could see people in lit windows, going about their lives as if nothing had happened. For them, I guess it hadn't. Nobody skulked or hid or dove out of view to avoid being seen. We'd even passed a guy walking his dog, and though he'd crossed the road to avoid the four grotty-looking kids, I couldn't help but be struck by the sheer normalcy of it all. Click had watched the dog until they'd turned a corner, then heaved a deep sigh.

"Are you sure this is the place?" Viktor asked, staring up at the rather large house.

"This is the address Dad gave me."

"I thought you were an only child. Why do they need so much space?"

She shook her head and stepped onto the sidewalk that led up to the front door. But instead of continuing forward, she veered off on another branch that led around the side of the house. We followed, walking single file, until we emerged onto a small patio. A door, embellished with a plastic wreath, was illuminated by a light on the wall.

"Oh," Viktor said, suddenly understanding.

"You think they're rich or something?" Niesha asked.

"Judging by your old house, yeah."

"That's where all their assets were tied up. The plan was to rent a basement suite until they were allowed back into Kenyonville."

"And then King Joshua burned down the place."

"Don't call him that," Niesha and I both said at the same time. Viktor held up his hands in surrender. "He's not a king," Niesha went on. "He's just a pissy little dick who's in way over his head. He can't even control his own minions."

"Did your folks have insurance?" Viktor asked.

"Of course. But it doesn't cover the Rift."

"The Rift didn't burn down the house. A couple of morons did."

She shook her head. "I don't know. I guess they'll look into it." Squaring herself in front of the door, she took a deep breath. "Here goes."

"Hope they're home," Viktor muttered as she reached for the doorbell.

"Shut up," she whispered, and then I heard what she obviously did: footsteps on the other side of the door. She took a step back as the door opened. The patio was flooded with light and a delicious aroma.

A man stood in the doorway. His bald head caught the light as he peered out at the four of us. But his gaze went almost immediately to Niesha and stuck there.

"Hey, Dad."

He said nothing, but stumbled over the threshold and grabbed her. She clung to him just as tightly, burrowing her face into his shoulder.

"Will, you're letting in bugs," a new voice said, and another figure appeared behind Niesha's dad. I could see the resemblance right away, even as her expression changed in understanding. Her hand flew to her mouth, and she bent over, again and again, like some sort of weird exercise. Niesha pulled away from her father and approached the woman, grabbing her from her crouch and pulling her up into her arms.

"You got out," her mom said, her tone one of disbelief.

"Oh, baby girl." Her dad reached out and ran his

hand over her fluffy ponytail, almost as if he still couldn't believe she was there.

"It's fine, Dad," she said. "I'm fine." She pulled back from her mom, who didn't seem to want to let go. The woman grabbed Niesha's face and pulled her close to kiss her cheek.

"We thought maybe you couldn't get out. It's been so long since you called."

"Only a few weeks. We would've tried to come sooner, but we needed to figure out how to do it."

Her dad shook his head. "I still can't believe they let you out. Did they come up with a vaccine?"

"It's not viral," she said, trying to look at him, but her mom was still kind of mauling her with love. I felt my heart twist as I watched the display of affection. "At least, that's what the doctor at the checkpoint said."

"But you're not affected anymore, are you?" her mom asked. "They wouldn't have let you out if you were."

"We're fine," Niesha said. "Whatever caused the glowing hands . . . it's gone now."

I frowned and glanced at Viktor. There were obviously a lot of things he and Niesha hadn't told me about the plan. Not that I would've voluntarily whipped out some Riftballs, but I would've liked to know what story they'd agreed to tell.

"That's right," her mom said, finally letting go of her and turning to the three of us who were still standing outside. "You said you were coming with friends." She looked us over carefully, one at a time, and her gaze stuck on Viktor. "Oh, you poor thing. What happened?"

"Don't let him start," Niesha said, "or you'll be sorry. He's fine, anyway." She paused to take in a deep breath. "What smells so good?"

"I was just making dinner," her dad said.

"Do you still cook way too much food?" Niesha asked. The man smiled.

"You know it, baby girl."

CHAPTER 12

FAMILY REUNION

’d never known food could taste so good. And Niesha's dad—Will—had made plenty. We sat in the living room, perched anywhere we could with bowls of hearty soup in hand while a plate of cornbread got passed around again and again. I wanted to keep eating and never stop, but I knew I had to be careful; my stomach was still recovering from months of near starvation, and I didn't want to push it too hard.

When we were all stuffed (and there were still plenty of leftovers), the room sort of devolved into a cozy party. At least, that was the best way I could describe it. Niesha's mom, Tammi, made sure she got the whole story: everything from the Week of Alarm to the destruction of their house. Will let Viktor borrow his laptop so he could try to track down his family. Click and I just curled up on the couch, watching the scene of enviable familial ease.

"I've lost all my followers," Viktor lamented, and when

I looked over at the laptop on the coffee table, I could see him scrolling through some sort of social media site.

"I thought you were looking up an address," Niesha said with a shake of her head. "Don't go getting readdicted on the first night."

"I'm not! But I thought maybe Noodle would be on here . . ."

"Who?" I asked.

"Ramona. My cousin." He screwed up his nose.

"You call her Noodle?"

"It started out as Ramen. Then it sort of morphed."

"Of course it did."

He frowned at the screen. "I would've thought she'd be all over this. Then again, she's only thirteen. Aunt Marlena might not have let her get an account yet."

"You don't think she has a secret one?" Niesha asked. Her dad raised his eyebrows.

"Did you have one when you were thirteen?"

"No." She shrugged sheepishly. "Fourteen."

He chuckled. "Not much we can do about it now."

"Actually," she said, "I miss all that crap less than I thought I would."

Viktor swiped at the trackpad, scrolling through his feed. "You don't miss your friends?"

"I never had that many. And the real ones . . ."

"That reminds me," Tammi said. "I ran into Leighton's mom the other day."

Niesha gaped. "Where?"

"The outlet mall over in Vandenberg." She nodded to herself as she stood up. "I told her you'd be getting out soon."

"Mom! You make it sound like I've been in jail."

"Haven't you?" Viktor asked absently. He frowned at the screen. "Dang."

"What do you expect?" Niesha asked him, shaking her head. "Your friends are probably all still stuck in the Rift Zone."

"Not my *online* friends."

"Those aren't friends."

"Obviously. Once they no longer had exposure to my dazzling wit, they unfollowed."

She snorted but sat up a little straighter when her mom reentered the room, phone in hand.

"I've got the number here somewhere," Tammi said, tapping at the phone as she sat back down. "Her mom said she got a new one." She handed the phone to Niesha, who just stared at it. "Be sure to congratulate her on the baby."

"What?" Niesha squeaked. "She had a baby? With who?"

"I didn't ask. She apparently got married last year."

"Jesus," Niesha whispered. She stared down at the phone, not really seeing it.

"How'd *that* happen?" Viktor asked. She shot him a dark look.

"You know how babies are made."

He shook his head. "Not that. I mean . . . how'd she get out of the Rift Zone?"

"She was never in the Rift Zone. I met her in one of my college classes. She lives over in Storram."

"Ah. Gotcha." He turned back to the laptop. "Oh, come on!"

"What?"

"I'm dead." He angled the laptop so she could see it. I caught a glimpse of a flashing image and leaned forward so I could see it better. It was some sort of memorial thing, with a bouquet of roses and animated sparkles. Text reading "Gone but not forgotten…" pulsed slowly in curly script.

"That's morbid," Niesha said.

"That's sick. If my aunt and uncle see this . . ." He sighed and logged out before transferring himself from the floor to the couch. Leaning back, he stretched his arm across my shoulders . . . until I turned and gave him the dirtiest look I could muster. "No sympathy for the dead guy? Oh, well." He pulled his arm away and sank into the cushions.

"So you didn't find an address?" Niesha asked. He shook his head. She bent over her mom's phone. "Give me a sec."

"A lot of evacuees ended up over at The Meadows," Will said.

Viktor frowned. "What's that?"

"A new development on the other side of town."

"Relatively new," Tammi added. "I think it was under construction when the Rift happened."

"There were obviously plenty of units still available," Will said. "I know of a few families who went there."

"Why didn't you go?" Niesha asked, somewhat distracted by the phone as she typed furiously with her thumbs.

"Because we didn't want to pay two mortgages. The Meadows doesn't have any rentals."

She looked up in surprise. "So . . . how are *they* affording two mortgages?"

"They're not. They most likely took advantage of the buyout." He rubbed a hand over his smooth head. "Plenty of people knew they wouldn't be going back to Kenyonville. So they've decided to settle here, at least until they can get their kids back."

"They're nice townhouses," Tammi added. "The Meadows. There's no reason not to stay."

Niesha sighed with a shake of her head. "You guys should've taken the offer. Or at least trusted someone else with your house."

Will grunted. "Who would you have suggested?"

"I don't know, Dad. Obviously not the daughter who let the place burn down."

"Don't worry, baby girl. I've already talked to the insurance broker. It's covered."

"Even though it's in the Rift Zone?"

He nodded. "The policy covers fire, floods, and other weather events."

"Does the Rift count?" Viktor asked.

"I doubt it. But this was arson."

Niesha frowned. "Arson's covered?"

"As long as they determine it wasn't one of us who

burned down the house. But I don't want you to worry about it, all right? It was just a house. This family is what's important."

Niesha's eyes got kind of shiny. She shoved the phone at Viktor as she stood up and crossed the room to her dad. As she squeezed herself onto the chair beside him, I couldn't help but feel a squeeze of envy in my chest. *I wonder what it's like to have a dad. Or a mom, for that matter. Ones that won't leave you . . .*

But they *had* left her, I reminded myself. Still, there was a difference between leaving a nineteen-year-old woman and a two-month-old baby. One already had the tools needed for survival. The other was entirely dependent on others.

Maybe I still was, even so many years later. I felt my throat tighten a little, but before my emotions could overtake me, Viktor let out a grunt of surprise.

"Found them!"

"*I* found them," Niesha mumbled, leaning into her dad's shoulder. "You're welcome."

"Unit seventeen, fourteen-eighty Meadows Muse."

"What did I tell you?" Will said.

Viktor set the phone down on the coffee table. "How long will it take to walk there?"

"Walk?" Tammi said, as if the thought were a completely bizarre one. "It's too late for that, hon." She thought for a moment. "How about if Will drives the three of you over there?"

Niesha lifted her head and stared at her mom in surprise. "Three?"

"You're not going anywhere, young lady. We just got you back."

"Mom. I'm twenty-two."

"You'll have plenty of time to hang out later. All the time in the world."

Niesha looked over at me, a frown growing. "But . . . Léa doesn't have anywhere to go. I thought . . ."

Tammi looked stricken. "Oh, baby. I'm sorry. We've only got one bedroom. As it is, you'll have to sleep on the couch."

"I'll sleep on the floor," Niesha said quickly. I shook my head and took a breath to say something, but Viktor jumped in first.

"It's fine. Léa can come with us." He turned to me. "You won't mind sharing a room with Ramona, will you?"

"No, but is she going to want to share with me?"

"She'll love you." He gave me a warm smile. I looked away. It wasn't the first time I'd felt unwanted, and it probably wouldn't be the last.

"It's temporary," I said, hating the way my cheeks were burning, and hating even more that I couldn't really put my finger on the emotion. "It's just until I find my own place." I raised my gaze to look at Niesha. "That was always the plan anyway, right?"

CHAPTER 13

COUSIN

t had been three years since I'd ridden in a vehicle. Properly. Not tossed in the back of a truck like a sack of potatoes.

Will drove a white SUV with grey leather seats and a sticker from a local college on the bumper. Viktor called shotgun (of course), leaving me and Click to climb into the back seats. Click seemed a little bewildered by the seatbelts, so I had to help him fasten his. He frowned down at the grey strap as if he had a snake across his lap.

The drive didn't take that long at all, and Viktor was quiet for most of it, which was weird. Then again, he was about to be reunited with his family. That was something I could only imagine.

The Meadows didn't look much like a meadow at all. There was a low brick wall, adorned with black metal letters, as we turned in to the complex. Beyond that, the streets were pretty bare. There wasn't much in the way of front yards, so the townhouses almost loomed over the street. Still, they looked clean and new from the outside, and probably weren't cheap, if their appearance was anything to go by.

"What unit was it again?" Will asked as he wove the SUV down the curving street, peering at the numbers affixed to decorative boulders that sat near the curb.

"Seventeen," Viktor said absently. He was busy looking out the window. "Did we miss it? We're up to fifty-seven on this side."

"There are two entrances," Will said, pulling his focus back to the road. "We technically came in the back way. The lower numbers are probably on the other end of the complex."

Viktor sighed. "Figures."

"It'll only take a minute to drive over there," Will said, speeding up a little. The streetlights cast moving shadows into the SUV as we passed them. I looked over at Click, who was staring at his lap.

"You okay?" I asked.

"What? Who?" Viktor twisted around in his seat. When he saw Click, he shook his head. "Look out the window, okay?"

I frowned. "Huh?"

"He looks like he's going to be sick."

"Try to hold on a little longer," Will said, sounding nervous. I didn't blame him. "We're almost there."

Click managed not to barf before Will pulled up in front of a unit whose rock had "17" on it. I unfastened his seatbelt and then, since it looked like he didn't know how to open his door, got out on my side and beckoned to him. He scrambled out, taking deep breaths. Viktor climbed out of the front seat and frowned down at his friend.

"Is he okay?" Will asked, leaning toward the passenger side.

"He should be," Viktor said. "I hope."

"You guys probably haven't been in a vehicle for three years, have you? It's going to take some time for your bodies to get used to that again."

"Yeah. Maybe." Viktor turned to him and bent down a little. "Thanks for the ride."

"You're very welcome."

"Tell Niesha we'll see her soon."

"Will do. It was nice to meet you," Will said, looking at Viktor, then at me. His gaze lingered for a moment on Click, who was staring up at the sky and gulping air. "Ginger ale should help," he said. "If you've got some."

"Thanks," Viktor said again. He closed the door and gave Will a little wave. The SUV pulled away, heading down the street. I watched its tail lights until it turned the corner. Then I turned back to Click.

"Do you want to sit down?" I asked. He didn't respond. Viktor placed a hand on his shoulder and looked into his face. The boy looked a little pale. And very sweaty.

"You feel like you're going to puke?" Viktor asked.

Click looked up at him, somewhat confused. "You know . . ." He made a sort of hurling noise and bent over, using his free hand to mime something coming out of his mouth. Click's face broke into a wavering smile.

"That was supposed to be puking?" I asked.

Viktor widened his eyes. "Are you mocking my acting skills?"

"What skills?"

With a snort, he tightened his hand on Click's shoulder and steered him toward the front door. "Come on. I want you guys to meet my family."

There was a little painted plaque beside the door with the words "Welcome Friends" surrounded by sunflowers. Below that, in the corner of the stoop, was a metal planter with some sort of ornamental grasses growing in it. A checkered doormat sat in front of the door, which had a wreath not unlike the one at Niesha's parents' suite. It certainly didn't seem like the sort of place where you'd live temporarily. Viktor's family appeared to have settled right in.

He stopped, the toes of his boots just brushing the edge of the doormat, and let his hand fall from Click's shoulder. I hovered behind them, waiting.

And waiting.

"Viktor?"

"Yeah. Just give me a sec." He reached up and tightened his ponytail, then smoothed back the strands on the sides that had escaped. Turning around, he fixed me with a gaze that looked almost desperate. "Do I look okay?"

"Define 'okay.'"

"Besides the melted face and cloudy eye."

The jabs came so automatically at that point that I didn't trust myself to speak. So I just nodded.

"Okay." He blew out a breath and turned back around. His shoulders seemed really tense. Without thinking too much about it, I reached forward and laid my hand gently on his back. He didn't say anything, but maybe it helped, just a little. He rang the doorbell.

Nothing happened.

We waited for what seemed like a really long time. It probably seemed even longer to Viktor. He jabbed his finger at the doorbell again, almost as if he thought it hadn't worked the first time. But we could all clearly hear the chime from within the house.

"Maybe they went out," I said slowly.

"All of them?" He shook his head. "Where would they go?"

"Out for dinner?"

He leaned forward, trying to peer through the window to the left of the door. It was covered by a sheer curtain, though, and we couldn't see much past it other than a bit of light.

"We can wait," I said, looking around for a place to do just that. The front lawns were tiny, but there was enough space for the three of us to sit. "It's getting late. They should be back soon."

But I didn't know if he'd heard me because, the next thing I knew, he was pounding his fist on the door.

"Aunt Marlena? Uncle Craig? It's me." He banged on the door again. I grabbed his arm.

"Stop it!"

"Why?"

"You're going to draw attention. And if someone calls the cops . . ."

"Why would they call the cops? Besides, if this is my aunt and uncle's place—"

"Your aunt and uncle aren't here right now," I snapped, "so there's no one to vouch for you. Or us. As far as anyone knows, we're just a trio of homeless kids looking for a place to break into."

"You think that's the conclusion they'd jump to?"

"Wouldn't you?"

"Not right away."

"Then what do you—" I broke off at the sound of the door opening. It was just a crack, not enough that we could really see inside. But the person standing on the other side could see out, and, as Viktor turned toward them, I heard a gasp. The door swung wider, revealing a girl. She looked about thirteen, with enviable dark hair that hung in shiny cascades over her shoulders. As she raised her eyebrows, I was overwhelmed by a sense of familiarity. The family resemblance was strong.

"Viktor?" the girl said, then sucked in another gasp as her gaze fell on the ruined side of his face. "Oh, my god." She started to cry. "Oh, my god."

Viktor chewed on his lip for a moment. Then he shook his head. "Nice to see you, too."

"What happened?" she shouted. Tears glistened in her dark eyes. She seemed almost angry. "What the fuck is going on?"

Viktor flinched, as if she'd slapped him. "Whoa. Where'd you learn that?"

"Yeah, Viktor, I swear. Get over it." She dashed the tears from her cheeks. "What happened to your face?"

"A Rift bear. Crawled right out of the Rift and decided to have a little snack." He pushed his cousin aside and strode into the house, leaving her gaping.

"Viktor!" I hissed.

He shook his head. "Come on in. It's my house, too."

"It is *not*," Ramona said. She edged back so Click and I could step into the space, staring at us warily the whole time.

"Are your parents home?" I asked. She turned all her attention on me, instantly suspicious.

"Yeah. Dad's upstairs cleaning his gun."

Viktor snorted as he turned around. "Yeah, right, Noodle. He doesn't even have a gun."

"He does now. What would you know? You've been gone for three years."

"You think that was my fault?"

"You're a Rifter."

"Again, do you think that was my fault? And besides, we're not Rifters anymore."

She blanched a little. "What?"

"Yeah. Don't know what happened, but . . ." He shrugged and raised his hands. "See? Nothing." He wiggled his fingers in her direction for emphasis, then dropped his arms to his sides. "So where *are* Aunt Marlena and Uncle Craig?"

Ramona didn't look like she wanted to answer any questions. She closed the front door without a word, then stormed toward the back of the house, leaving us standing in the rather cramped foyer. A staircase disappeared into the second level. A few steps away, a doorway led into a more open space that appeared to be lit. Viktor stared after his cousin, but then he sighed and tiptoed toward the doorway. Click and I followed.

The living room looked like a cross between a show home and the cluttered house where we'd found Buddy. Not that it was dirty; the place looked spotless, and I couldn't see so much as a speck of dust on any surface. But the space was small, and it looked like more than one family had crammed their stuff into it, resulting in kind of a weird aesthetic. There was a TV mounted on the wall above the fireplace, sort of blocked by a bunch of knickknacks: figurines, a rack of souvenir spoons, some dried flowers in a vase.

"Aunt Marlena's always been sentimental," Viktor said when he noticed me looking. He peered past the fireplace to the stuffed bookcase on the far side of the room.

"Your family brought a lot of stuff with them," I said, keeping my voice low.

"They didn't. Aunt Marlena used the evacuation as an excuse to declutter. A lot of this stuff is new." He shook his head and tiptoed over to read the spines. "*Vampires in Montpelier. The Harvest Moon of Babylon. Once Upon a Raptor.*" He let out a snort. "What the fart are these?"

"Um . . . those are called books. I thought you were some sort of child genius."

He turned to me with a withering look. "I never read that kind of—" He broke off, and his eyes widened as he stared at something behind me. I edged out of the way as I turned, coming face to face with . . . well, the only way I could describe it would be a shrine. A small table had been set up in the corner of the room, covered in a dark red cloth. A collection of unlit votive candles and wilting chrysanthemums surrounded a single photograph in a frame. I stepped closer and bent over to get a better look.

There was a weird sensation in my stomach as I peered at the picture. It had to have been taken at least three years earlier. Probably more, judging by the fact that the kid had braces. He didn't seem that bothered by them, either, the way he was smiling and showing them off. The self-assuredness in his expression was achingly familiar; I'd seen it plenty over the last few weeks. What wasn't familiar, though, was the deep (and rather adorable) dimple in his left cheek, and the mischievous sparkle in both dark eyes that were rimmed by thick lashes. His hair was shorter, but still long enough to swoop over his forehead in a trendy style. When I straightened up and looked back at Viktor, he was chewing on his lip again.

"Long lost twin," he said.

"Really?"

He collapsed onto the couch, then tugged a crocheted blanket out from under his butt. "Spit."

"At least you know they care."

He shook his head. "That's not even me. That's my cousin. He died a few years ago."

"Oh." I looked back at the photo. "That's one heck of a family resemblance."

"No kidding. We might as well have been twins. Right down to the dimple and the farting braces." He stared at the photo for a few seconds. "Good thing I got the train tracks off the week before the Rift, eh? That would've been a bunny." He bit his lip again and looked away, focusing his gaze on the bookcase once more. "This is going to fart everything up," he muttered.

"What are you talking about?"

He blinked up at the odd collection of books, as if lost in thought. "You think I can just step back into this life?"

"Why not?"

"You don't get it."

"No, I don't get it. You have a family, Viktor. I don't see what—" I broke off at the sound of footsteps. Ramona returned, holding a piece of paper. She cast a nervous glance at Click, who was standing in the doorway, looking more pallid than ever, then turned to her cousin.

"This is where they are," she said, holding the paper out toward him. He sat forward to take it, frowning. She watched, her gaze fixed on the left side of his face. "What happened to you out there?"

"*In* there," he corrected her, unfolding the paper and giving it a quick scan. "Are you farting serious?" When he looked up at her again, his expression was a mixture of hurt and anger. My heart quickened.

"What is it?" I whispered.

He tossed the paper onto the coffee table (which was already almost invisible thanks to its many layers of magazines) and shook his head. "They're at a support group."

"For what? Bereavement?"

"No." He almost spat the word. Ramona took a step back. I wanted to, too. Anger was not something I'd really seen Viktor wear, and it didn't suit him. "It's a support group for the families of Rifters."

I shook my head, frowning. "Yeah . . . They'll all be going through the same thing. What's so—"

"They left us in there," he said, standing so abruptly that his cousin took another step back. "They abandoned us in that heckhole, and then they pretend they're some sort of victims."

"That's not—" Ramona began, but he threw up his hands. It was just to get her to stop talking—I understood that much—but the effect it had was more dramatic. She let out a shrill scream and threw her forearms over her face.

"Stop it, Viktor!" I shouted, the words coming out automatically. He turned to me in disbelief, his hands still raised.

"Stop what? Being angry? Don't you think I have a right to be?"

"You're scaring your cousin."

"There's no reason to be scared," he said. He slowly lowered his hands. Ramona sucked in a breath that sounded like a hiccup.

"How many people have you killed?" she asked, her voice small from behind the fists that were still covering her face. Viktor blanched.

"What?"

"How many?" She pulled her fists down so she could better see him. "We know that's what happens in there."

"Who's 'we'?"

She gave the tiniest of shrugs.

"Noodle, who's 'we'?"

"The other kids at school."

"You going to listen to a bunch of prepubescent donkeybutts?"

She let her hands fall a little more so she could shoot him a dark look. "What's the matter with you? Why don't you talk like a *normal* person?"

"Like the other kids at school?" He narrowed his eyes at her. "You think they know everything?"

"Some of them have older brothers and sisters in the Rift Zone. So, yeah. We know."

"You know what goes on in a place you've never even seen?"

"I remember what it was like."

"No, you don't. You left before things got apocalyptic. So don't stand there and tell me you know what it's like. You don't get to stand there and tell me we're a bunch of murderers." His voice was getting loud. Click stepped forward and tried to grab his arm, but he wrenched away, still staring at Ramona. "I'm not dead!" he shouted. "They left me in there, and I survived, but they don't even care. It's easier to have a dead kid than a Rifter. Is that it?"

Ramona just stared at him, her eyes wide. Viktor stood there, trembling, his eyes glistening with tears. I had an urge to step over there and give him a hug, but I honestly didn't know how it would be received. So I just stayed where I was, holding my breath, as I watched some sort of silent war go on in his head.

"Vee-kah," Click said, startling all of us. Viktor turned to him, and the mask of anger evaporated.

"Spit," he said, bending down to look Click in the eye. "What's wrong?"

Click raised a shaking hand and pressed it over his chest. "Ree-fah."

"Yeah, we'll get you home. But we have to figure out where that is first."

Click sagged a little, his legs wobbling. Viktor grabbed his arm just as the boy collapsed to the floor.

"Get him a glass of water!" Viktor cried. "Or . . . ginger ale. Do you have any?"

"What's wrong with him?" Ramona asked. "Is it the virus?"

"There is no virus," Viktor said, then shook his head. "It doesn't matter. Just get something wet." He knelt down beside Click, rubbing his hand over the boy's back. "Breathe, okay?"

Click's breaths were hitching. He pressed his hand harder over his chest, his face twisted in pain.

"What's going on?" I asked as Ramona returned with a glass of water. She handed it to Viktor and quickly backed away.

"Heck if I know. Here. Have a sip." He held the glass to steady it as Click brought it to his mouth. Droplets leaked out around his lips with the violent trembling.

"He hasn't looked right since we left the checkpoint," I said. "But he was fine this morning." I frowned. "Do you think it's the epi?"

"I don't see why it would be. It should be out of our systems by now."

"Food poisoning?" I asked, then shook my head. "No. It started before we had dinner."

"Could've been something else," Viktor said. "But we've all been eating the same things."

"Why don't you just ask him?" Ramona said, her voice small.

"Because he doesn't speak English."

"Then how do you communicate?"

"We manage." He gave Click a gentle pat on the back. "You okay?"

But Click didn't give a thumbs up. I'd never seen him complain about anything in all the time I'd been with them. So he had to have been feeling pretty awful.

"Well, other than severe homesickness," Viktor said, "I'm not sure what else it would be."

"Wouldn't that have happened years ago when he first got trapped in the Rift Zone?" I asked.

He sighed. "I don't know." His teeth went back to his lip. His gaze flicked around the room, then settled on the shrine. His expression hardened. "Come on. Get up." He stood, grabbing Click's arm. I took the other side, and we managed to pull him to his feet. And then Viktor started to walk. I just followed along, bewildered, as we went back through the foyer and headed for the front door.

"Viktor?" Ramona began. "Where are you going?"

He pulled open the door and steered Click through it. I went with them, keeping a tight grip on Click's arm; I could still feel him shaking.

"Viktor, you can't just—"

He let go of Click and turned, stepping back toward his cousin. She backed up and then stopped, staring up at him. "I have to go," he said, his voice holding a soft devastation that I'd never heard before . . . and that I hoped I would never have to hear again. I gripped Click's arm and watched them, feeling my heart squeeze.

"But you just got back."

"No, I didn't. I was never here. Okay?" He reached out and placed a gentle hand on her shoulder. "I'm not the same person I was three years ago. He's dead. And I don't know if you're going to be able to let the new Viktor into your lives."

"We will!" she protested. "Viktor, please. Mom will—"

"Aunt Marlena will cry when she sees me. And she'll blame herself."

"So what?" she said, her voice taking on an edge of desperation. "They already blame themselves for leaving you in there. But you're here now, and that's all that matters."

"It's not all that matters, Noodle." He let go of her shoulder, then gave it a gentle nudge with his fist. "Promise me something?"

"What?"

"Don't tell them I was here."

"But—"

"Please. It'll just hurt them all over again." He shook his head and took a step back. "I have to go."

"Viktor . . ."

"Promise me."

"I can't."

"Yes, you can. You're an only child now. Enjoy it."

He stepped back and turned around, coming to join us once more.

"Asshole!" she shouted, then let out a sob. "Why would you do this to Mom and Dad?"

"I'm not doing anything," he said, casting his words over his shoulder. "If you keep your promise, they'll never know I was here."

"I never promised." She took another step forward and grasped the doorframe. "You're going to break their hearts."

"No," he said, pausing so he could look back at her. "You are, if you tell them. It's time to let go, all right? What was born in the Rift Zone is meant to stay there." He turned and strode forward, so fast that Click and I almost couldn't keep up.

The door slammed behind us. I looked up at Viktor, whose jaw was set.

"Do you really want to leave it like that?" I asked, my voice low.

He stared up into the night sky, as if he were trying to keep tears from falling. "Let's just get out of here before my aunt and uncle get home, okay?"

CHAPTER 14

THE HARDEST CHOICE

I don't want to go back. I don't want to go back. I don't want to go back!

The refrain kept up as we walked through The Meadows, heading back the way we'd come. Click was still sagging between us, his steps shuffling, his breathing pained. But with Viktor on one side and me on the other, he was steady enough to keep walking, albeit slowly.

We'd almost made it back to the entrance of the complex when a car passed us. Viktor sucked in a breath and turned his head away, wincing.

"What?" I asked.

"My aunt and uncle."

I craned my neck and looked behind us. The car wasn't stopping.

"Did they see me?" he asked.

"They probably saw you. Doesn't look like they recognized you."

"Twelve inches and half a face can have that effect."

"You have a face. It's just . . ."

"Melted?"

I turned to him with a frown, peering at him over the top of Click's curly head. The good side was toward me, and Niesha's words suddenly made sense. Viktor was hot. Or, he would've been, if he hadn't damaged himself. I thought back to the photograph of the thirteen-year-old doppelgänger. The lost dimple. I could almost imagine it now, popping into existence with that cheeky smile.

Although, that was something I hadn't seen in a while.

"Forget it, Léa."

"What?"

"You're trying to think of something to say to make me feel better. It's fine. You don't have to."

"I feel like I should. I . . . haven't exactly been kind about it."

He glanced at me, and the soft smile on his lips buoyed my heart a little. "At least my teeth are straight, right?"

"Um . . . but they're not."

"Yeah. Kind of lost my retainer in the chaos." He sighed. "Oh, well. It's not like a dazzling smile would've cancelled out the rest of it, right?"

I didn't say anything. We continued on into the night.

Click was so wobbly that we eventually gave up. We stumbled into a park with a pretty impressive play structure and collapsed on the grass near the bottom of the slide. Click curled into a ball and closed his eyes, leaving Viktor and I to exchange a worried glance.

"Motion sickness?" I suggested.

"He wouldn't still be feeling this sick." Folding his long legs, he settled himself on the grass, staring at his friend.

"He might," I said. "If he's not used to cars."

"None of us are used to cars anymore."

I shook my head. "He didn't seem to know what a seatbelt was."

"Maybe they're not big on using them wherever he's from." He shrugged and turned away, staring off over the expanse of grass. In the Rift Zone, such a park might've had a few people sleeping in it, especially at this time of year. But the place was deserted. And eerily still. There wasn't even enough of a breeze to move the swings.

"So . . ." I began hesitantly. He turned to me, eyebrows high. "What's the plan?"

He didn't answer. It was almost like he didn't even understand the question.

"You can still go back to your aunt and uncle's place. Once you cool off."

He snorted. "You don't think I'm cool?"

"I think storming out of the only proper family you have is very uncool."

His mouth twisted in a wry grin. "Thanks."

"Ramona was right, you know. You made it out of the Rift Zone. That's all that matters. You're alive, and your family is here, so you should take advantage of it."

He lay back on the grass with a sigh. "You saw her reaction to my face."

"She was just . . . surprised."

"Aunt Marlena's reaction would be a thousand times worse." He laced his fingers together over his stomach. "I don't even know what Uncle Craig would say."

"You're assuming. You know what would probably happen? They'd grab you and hug you and never let you go. Because that's what parents—even adoptive parents—do."

He rolled his head toward me with a frown. "How do you know what parents do? I thought you said—"

"Shut up," I snapped.

"Okay." He held up his hands for a moment. "Sorry."

I threw my arms around my middle and held on tight. Despite the fact that it was summer, the night air wasn't very warm. Even my jacket wasn't doing that great of a job. "I don't get it," I said, my voice coming out tainted with misery. "You have an aunt and an uncle and a cousin. And you're sitting out here in a stupid park, expecting me and Click to fill in for them."

"That's not what I'm doing."

"Yeah, it is. Do you expect us to just stay with you forever? Once we find out where Click belongs, he'll go home. And I'm not going to hang around and be your girlfriend, or whatever it is you think—"

"Whoa. Who said anything about that?" He raised himself up on one elbow so he could frown at me. "When have I ever—"

"You talk about it. All the time. Repopulating the Rift Zone. Shit like that."

"I thought you knew me better than that."

"Huh?"

"They're just jokes, Léa." He lay back down with a sigh. "Stupid ones, apparently."

"Yeah, they are." I gripped my jacket in both hands and looked over at Click. He was really still, and his eyes were closed, but I could see him breathing.

"Pretty, isn't he?"

I blinked and turned to Viktor, who was staring up into the sky. "I guess."

He smirked. "Prettier than me."

"Everybody's prettier than you." The words were automatic. I bit my lips together. "Sorry."

"Why are you sorry? It's the truth." He closed his eyes. "What does it really matter, anyway? It's not like I need to attract a mate."

"Then how is the Rift Zone Repopulation Agenda supposed to work?"

He rolled his head toward me as he opened his eyes. "You think the Rift Zone is a great place to have a baby?"

"Some people have done it."

"Yeah. Not on purpose, I hope." His mismatched gaze flickered over my body. "Are you shivering?"

"No," I lied, but even that small syllable held a bit of a quaver. He crooked his finger at me.

"Come here."

"I'm not spooning you."

He let out a grunt of laughter. "I'm not asking you to. Side by side, hands to ourselves. It won't help a ton, but it'll be something."

"Are you cold?"

"I'm not *not* cold."

I hesitated for a moment, then scooted closer. As I lay back on the grass, I could feel the coolness of the ground seeping through my jacket. But there was a line of warmth where our arms touched that felt kind of nice.

"Better?" he asked.

"As long as you keep your hands to yourself."

"Don't I always?"

"No."

He chuckled, then let out a sigh.

"You never answered my question earlier," I reminded him.

"About what?"

"What we're going to do now."

"It's not like we have a ton of options. Niesha's folks don't have room for us. My family's out."

"They shouldn't be."

"We don't have money to get a hotel room," he

went on as if I hadn't spoken. "And I suspect it'll be kind of tricky for me to get a job."

"Why? Don't people like hiring geniuses?"

He snorted. "What do you get when you cross a genius with a hideous scar?"

"I don't know."

He turned to me, eyebrows raised. "A supervillain."

"Since when?"

"Since forever. Pick up any comic book. Watch a few movies."

"You're not a fictional character."

He rolled his eyes. "I know that. But my appearance is certainly not going to help when people have all these biases programmed into them from the media they consume."

"Are you planning on applying for a job at a high-security military facility or something? Because I'm pretty sure you couldn't do much damage working at Waffle Loft."

He laughed. "Oh, man. Remember their Ladder Stack?"

"I've never been."

He sucked in a breath of disbelief. "Are you serious? You've never had that glorious tower of waffles, bacon, maple syrup, and cheese?"

"Cheese?" I asked, making a face.

"Yeah. I know. Sounds weird, but it's actually really good. My parents used to take me there for my birthday. I'd look forward to it all year."

"You would."

"I'll have you know, I have a very refined palate."

"Sounds like it."

He shook his head on the grass. "I'll take you sometime."

"That sounds suspiciously like you're asking me out."

"Maybe I am."

"I thought we weren't doing . . . that. Besides," I said before he could go on, "Waffle Loft has been closed for three years."

"It might open again. One day."

I sighed. "You really think they'll ever open up the Rift Zone?"

"They might. If they realize there's no more threat."

"But there is."

"Not necessarily. We learned to control our powers."

I snorted. "Powers."

"What else would you call them? My point is that pinkhands can be controlled. We're proof of that."

"But we're the only ones who can do it."

"We're the only ones who've *tried* to do it," he corrected me. "Most of the kids in there are probably like us. They're just trying to survive, waiting for the day when the nightmare will be over. They don't realize they could wake up from it like"—he snapped his fingers for emphasis—"that."

"So . . ."

He looked at me, and I felt my heart sink.

"We can't go back," I said.

"Why not?"

"Um . . . because those guards with the guns aren't going to let us back in."

"They would if we showed them our pinkhands."

I gaped at him. "Are you serious? That's a great way to get shot."

"They wouldn't shoot us. Not on the outside where someone might hear it."

"Oh, that's reassuring."

"Do you really want to leave everybody stuck in there, not realizing they have the power to get out?"

"Okay, first of all," I said, rolling onto my side so I could glare at him better, "do you really think the military is just going to let all the Rifters walk out of there? There's no way all of them would pass the test."

"Some of them would."

"And some of them wouldn't. They'd get turned away."

He chewed on his lip for a moment, then took a deep breath. "So you'd rather everybody in there had no hope at all?"

"I didn't say that."

"But you don't want to help."

"I don't want to go back!" My voice was too loud. He blinked at me in surprise. "Why should I do anything for any of them? All they've done is cheat, steal, kill—"

"Whoa. Kill?" His eyes widened. "Who was killed?"

"Nobody," I said, rolling onto my back. I was no

longer touching him, and the few inches between us felt like a sea of ice. "It doesn't matter."

"That sounded like two big lies in a row."

"Fuck off."

He sighed. "One day, you'll talk to me."

"Arrogant prick. Don't tell me what I'm going to do."

"One day, you'll let me in. And when that day comes, I'll understand."

"No, you won't," I said. I rolled away from him and grasped a handful of grass. The blades felt strong, even though I was pulling hard, trying to break them before the dam of my emotions gave way.

CHAPTER 15

RETURN

awoke to an aching-cold damp. The early grey light bathed the world in a monochrome palette. My back muscles were stiff, and I realized I was shivering like crazy. Pushing myself up to a sitting position, I took stock of my surroundings.

The park was still quiet. It was far too early for anyone to be using it for the normal things like playing or exercising or relaxing. So there was no one around.

There was no one around.

A surge of panic drove itself all the way into my fingertips, and I sprang to my feet. Thankfully, my hands weren't flaring, but that didn't make me feel much better. I turned in a circle, searching for any sign of Viktor or Click.

Oh, my god. Did they leave me here? I know I said I didn't want to go back, but I didn't mean I wanted to be abandoned here all by myself. What am I supposed to do? Should I go back to Viktor's family's house? No . . . too many questions. Especially if Viktor and Click aren't there. I'd have to come up with some elaborate story, and Ramona would have to go along with it. If I go back to Niesha's . . . No. I can't do that, either. Her parents are obviously content with the one kid.

I sank down into a crouch, my hands on my head, as I tried to quell my rising panic. For some reason, being stranded alone in boringly normal Goldvale was a hell of a lot worse than being stranded alone in unpredictable Kenyonville. I'd spent months on my own there. So why did the prospect of being alone now scare me so bad?

"And you say *I'm* uncouth," Viktor's voice said, and I twisted my head around so fast that it kind of hurt my neck. I spotted him approaching from across the grassy field, Click ambling slowly behind him.

"Where were you?" I shouted. He drew up, coming to a stop with a look of surprise on his face. He pointed back over his shoulder to a small building couched between some trees and shrubbery.

"Bathroom. Didn't think it would be polite to just squat in the field." He raised his eyebrows, and I realized what he meant. I quickly stood up.

"I wasn't doing *that*," I said, my cheeks flooding with embarrassment.

"Sure." His cheeky smile was back in place as he strode forward once more.

"I wasn't. You think I'm going to do that through my jeans?"

"Hey," he said, holding up his hands, "I'm not going to judge your bathroom habits." He came to a stop beside me and looked down. "So. You coming with us?"

"Where? Back to hell?"

"Yeah. See, I've been thinking."

"I'm shocked."

He chuckled and started to walk again, this time heading for the street. I glanced at Click—who was still kind of pale, but not as bad as the day before—and jogged after Viktor.

"You want to slow down a bit? We can't all have legs that are five feet long."

He snorted. "Your estimate is way off."

"I was exaggerating to make a point," I said, reaching out to grab his sleeve and hold him back a little. "What's the rush?"

He slowed down—marginally—and glanced back to make sure Click was still with us. Satisfied, he nodded. "We need to keep moving. I don't want to end up crossing through Permanent Marc's territory in the dark."

The name sent a shudder through me. "Why does that stupid checkpoint have to be in *his* territory?"

"Luck. Bad luck." He shook his head. "Doesn't matter. The point is that we need to keep moving."

"Why are you so eager to go back? Have you forgotten what it was like?"

"Nope. Which is why I want to get back there." He turned and looked down at me. In the early morning light, his cloudy eye looked pale and eerie. "Everything happens for a reason."

I frowned. "Not always a good reason."

"True. But, in this case, I think it did."

"What are you talking about?"

"This." He made a vague motion with his hand. "Coming here. Getting rejected."

"We didn't," I pointed out. "Not at your place, anyway."

He shook his head. "I don't think we were supposed to stay here."

"Then what were we supposed to do?"

"Get out. And . . . get it."

"Get what?"

He came to a sudden stop. Click and I both did the same.

"I thought you wanted to keep moving," I said, but before I could say anything else, he made his little raspberry noises, raising his hands at the same time. Nothing happened. I frowned. "What do pinkhands have to do with—"

"Léa, pay attention."

"I am! I just don't see—"

"Exactly. Try it."

"What the fuck? I'm not trying it. If someone sees . . ."

He raised his eyebrows high. I shook my head slowly. "Viktor, I'm not—"

"Do you feel it?"

"Feel what?"

"Close your eyes."

I let out a growl under my breath, but I did as he said. *The sooner he makes his point, the sooner we can . . . do whatever it is we're going to do.*

"Now, sense the Rift energy. Feel it flowing down your arms."

"I . . ." I began, then trailed off. My hands felt strange. Lighter. Softer. It was an odd sensation, but it also felt sort of familiar. Because I'd felt it before.

I remembered it from before.

"Holy shit," I said, opening my eyes and raising my right hand in front of me. It should've been flaring a bright pink, but it wasn't. It looked like a regular hand. Just like the hands Viktor was holding up in front of himself, cupping the air as if he were holding a couple of invisible Riftballs. "How did *that* happen?"

"Remember what Doc Frazier said? What creates a Rifter?"

"Hormones, brain development, and . . ." My breath caught as I looked up at him.

"Proximity to the Rift," he finished.

My eyes were so wide, it felt like they might drop right out of my skull. "Do they know?"

"What? Who?"

"The military. The people who kept us trapped in there. Do they know that they could've just evacuated all of us, and Rifters wouldn't have been an issue?"

His bright expression wavered for a moment at that thought. "I don't know. But," he said, dropping his hands and striding forward once more, "if they don't, we can show them. We can end this today."

"If they believe you," I muttered, hurrying to catch up.

"Why wouldn't they?"

"Um . . . because we lied to get out of there, for one thing. The doctor knows that. We haven't exactly given her a reason to trust us."

He waved his hand as if he were shooing a pesky fly.

"So what's your plan? You're just going to walk up to them, tell them they need to evacuate all the kids to cure them, and they'll just do it? I don't think it's going to be that simple."

"Maybe not." He reached back to tighten his ponytail. "We'll do it in stages, then. Teach as many kids as we can how to pass the test. Then, when enough of them are out, there'll be plenty of proof that getting away from the Rift is the cure. The military won't have any excuse to keep anyone inside the Rift Zone anymore."

"They're the military," I said. "They have the weapons and the walls. They can do whatever the hell they want. And Rifters are still Rifters while they're inside the Rift Zone. Why would the military give them a free pass?"

"Because you can't imprison someone over what they *might* do. Heck, I could bludgeon someone with a syrup decanter from Waffle Loft. That doesn't mean I should be imprisoned because I have the potential to commit murder with a condiment."

"And yet," I said, shrugging for emphasis. He shook his head.

"It might take some time to convince them. It's not going to happen overnight. They've operated under the assumption that we're a feral mass of donkeybutts for the last three years. They need the opportunity to shift their paradigms."

I snorted. "I never thought I'd hear 'feral mass of donkeybutts' and 'shift their paradigms' in the same speech."

"Is that a good thing or a bad thing?"

"It's a weird thing," I said, casting a glance at him out of the corner of my eye. He smiled and looked down at the ground in front of us. "Say we do this," I went on. "If we go back . . . what will we do? Niesha's not there anymore to protect you."

"Katja likes me. I'm sure we can work something out."

"Bah-dee," Click said, and we both turned to look at him. He was trudging along beside us gamely, though he still looked kind of pale.

"Yeah, I guess we can pick up Buddy on the way," Viktor said, throwing his arm around Click's shoulders. "I kind of miss the smelly little guy."

"He wouldn't smell if you guys bathed him," I said.

"I don't think he'd like a cold bath any more than I would."

"About that," I said. "You need to shift your paradigms about showering."

He chuckled. "Excuse me?"

"You're ripe."

"Gosh, Léa. You sure know how to build a guy's self-esteem." He raised his free arm to sniff his pit. "I don't smell anything."

"I swear," I muttered. "You couldn't have a worse sense of smell if Buddy had eaten your nose."

—

By the time we made it to the downtown area of Goldvale, the sun was high overhead and the whole place was bustling. Given that it was summer, there were lots of kids of all ages out and about, doing whatever it was that normal kids did: hanging out with their friends, heading to the air-conditioned theatre to see a matinée, wandering aimlessly with lots of laughter while holding frosty drinks. I ended up taking off my jacket and tying the sleeves around my waist, leaving my t-shirt with its pit stains on full display. That was the least of the reasons I was embarrassed, though. The teenagers seemed to have some sort of radar, like they knew we were different. Every time we'd pass some, they'd go really quiet, only to start up again with renewed laughter as soon as they'd moved along.

"Ladies," Viktor said to a group of three girls as they edged past us. One of them wouldn't even look at him. The other two stared, gaping at his face. They turned away quickly enough, though not without exchanging a look.

"Shouldn't we keep a low profile?" I asked. He shrugged, then pulled off his jacket, bunching it up so he could carry it in one hand.

"I'm just being friendly."

"You're scaring the villagers. Why do you think they're all whispering?"

"They're probably wondering how someone like me managed to land someone like you."

"Shut up."

He grinned.

"They're probably whispering because they can't believe how bad you reek. I mean, you *look* normal enough, but . . ."

"But what?"

I grunted. "You need to ask? You haven't showered in two weeks. And it's been hot, so you've been sweating."

"So've you."

I blinked at him in disbelief. But he just chuckled and nudged my arm with the fist that was holding the jacket.

"I promise: First thing I do when we get home is take a shower."

"With soap."

"Oh, come on!"

"Soap," I said, fixing him with a glare. "If I have to share a basement with you again, I want to be able to breathe."

—

wanted to keep moving and get away from all the judgmental stares, but Viktor had other ideas. As we strolled down the summer-busy streets, a plethora of delicious aromas hit us from all sides, and I understood what he was probably after. Sidewalk patios were stuffed with noisy, laughing diners. We wouldn't have found a place to sit if we'd tried. Not that anyone was about to let us into their establishment. We might've had shirts and shoes, but we also stank of many things, the least of which was desperation. I hung back with Click as Viktor led us down the street (a futile attempt to pretend I didn't know the tall, smelly teenager), all while diners pretended not to notice the three haggard kids who probably looked like they'd just stepped off the set of a post-apocalyptic movie.

As we got farther from the centre of town, the restaurants changed from swanky bistros and gastropubs to cookie-cutter fast-food places and food trucks on the edges of strip-mall parking lots. I started to relax a little when I could no longer feel so many gazes upon me.

"What do you feel like?" Viktor called back over his shoulder.

"You got money?"

"Yeah. It's in my wallet." He made a show of patting his jeans pockets with his free hand. "Fart. Someone must've stolen it."

"I'm not in the mood."

"For what?"

"You."

He chuckled as he stopped at the corner and waited for us to catch up. "Hangry again?"

"I could eat. But—"

"So, let's eat."

"How do you propose we do that?"

He pointed at the fast-food place on the other side of the crosswalk.

"Yeah . . . My question stands."

He straightened up a little and looked down at me with a haughty tilt of one eyebrow. "Are you underestimating my charm again?"

"You're going to beg?"

"No, I'm going to charm."

"Great. We're going to starve."

He grunted and moved his jacket to his other hand so he could press the button for the walk signal. "I would never let that happen." The last word was drowned out by a mechanical chirping noise that made both of us jump. It had been years since I'd heard that sound.

The three of us headed through the crosswalk, passing a group of people who gave us such a wide berth that I was afraid they were going to get hit by the traffic in the intersection. When we stepped onto the sidewalk, Viktor turned to the right, seeming to head for the drive-thru.

"Where are you going?"

"I'm going where the food is. Where are *you* going?"

"You don't have a car."

He shook his head. "We don't need a car."

"But—"

"Just trust me, okay?"

"Are you going to make us eat out of a dumpster?"

He pointed to the bin in question as we rounded the side of the building. It appeared to be locked. So I kept my mouth shut and just followed him. The parking lot opened up in front of us, and the heat radiating off the asphalt was uncomfortably warm. Most of the parking spots around the fast-food place were occupied, and the drive-thru had a line of cars snaking around one side of the building. The outdoor seating area was packed, but that wasn't surprising; there was some sort of food truck parked nearby, with a healthy-looking lineup just outside its window. Viktor finally stopped and turned to me.

"What'll we have? Burgers or tacos?"

"Are you planning on robbing a food truck?"

"No. Are you?"

"What do you think?"

He shrugged. "You're kind of unpredictable when you're hangry, so . . ."

"Shut up."

"Kind of a bunny, too."

"Viktor, I swear—"

"You do swear a lot," he said with a grin that made me want to punch him. Seeming to realize that he was about to turn this bunny rabid, he shook his head and walked over to an empty bench that was conveniently situated right between the seating area and the food truck. I had no idea why it was empty . . . until I sat down on it. The metal surface, after sitting in direct sunlight for hours, was uncomfortably hot through my jacket and jeans.

"Not very bright," Viktor muttered, standing up again so he could lay his jacket on the bench.

"Did you design it?"

"Despite what you think, I'm not *that* stupid." With a sigh, he flopped down beside me.

"Why are we sitting here?" I asked, glancing at Click, who didn't seem to have any problem with the heat of the bench through his jeans and skirt.

"You're hungry, aren't you?"

"Yeah, but I don't see any food here."

"Just wait."

"For what?"

He leaned back and stretched his long legs out, crossing his ankles.

"I thought you were going to use your charm."

"You were probably right about that."

"Yeah. You're not charming."

"Oh, I'm charming. But I might not have quite enough charm to overcome the scar."

I opened my mouth to tell him not to forget about his cloudy eye, then closed it again. *Stop it, Léa. Be nice.* Easier said than done when he was being annoyingly mysterious and all I could think about was my stomach.

"Look," he said, keeping his voice low. My gaze snapped toward a man in the seating area who was weaving his way between the tables, a trash-piled tray in hand, a couple of kids trailing behind. He slid the empty wrappers off the tray and into the trash, then left the tray on top of the bin before grabbing the hand of the smaller kid and strolling out into the parking lot.

"Um . . . did you see the same thing I did?" I asked. "I'm not eating a paper wrapper."

"I'm not asking you to. But someone's going to leave more than a wrapper on their tray."

"How does that help—" I began, but stopped when I saw a young woman approach the trash can from the direction of the food truck. In her hand was a little cardboard bowl. And it was not empty.

"Gosh," Viktor said loudly, causing me to startle a little, "I sure am hungry. Too bad I lost my wallet."

I wanted to crawl under the bench. And when the woman turned to look at us, I wanted to lift up a corner of the parking lot and slide myself underneath. She stared at Viktor, still walking, then turned to me. I thought she was going to say something. Maybe offer us the half taco (or whatever it was) that I could see inside that little white bowl. She raised her eyebrows.

"Go," Viktor whispered, and despite the shame

that was making my skin prickle with heat, I stood up. But before I could take a single step, the woman smiled at me . . . and tossed the bowl into the trash.

My mouth went dry, even as my eyes threatened to get very wet. I'd never actually cried about being hungry—I hadn't cried about anything, really, not for years—but something about what I'd just seen was too much. I stared at the garbage bin as I sank back down onto the bench.

"Whoa. What a bunny."

"Can we just go home now?" I asked, my voice miserable.

"I thought you were hungry."

I looked down at my lap. The next thing I knew, Viktor's arm was around my shoulders. The weather was really too hot for that sort of thing, so I shrugged away. "Don't."

"Want me to see if I can salvage it?" he asked as he reached back and gave his ponytail a quick tug.

"What? Our dignity?"

"Huh?"

"I'm not eating out of the trash."

"The food might not have touched anything gross."

"And it might have touched a bag of dog poop."

"I don't think they serve dog poop here."

"Oh, my god, Viktor." I leaned over, putting my head in my hands. His hand settled on my back for a moment, gave it a quick rub, then lifted as he stood. I just stayed where I was, hunched over in hungry misery, and watched his boots move away. I closed my eyes, but all I could think about was that partial taco languishing in the darkness of the bin. *Maybe he's right. If it's still in the bowl, it's probably fine. And if it's just food wrappers in there, it's still edible. You don't have the luxury of being picky anymore.*

It seemed like Viktor was gone for a long time, but it was probably only a few minutes. When I heard his footsteps, I lifted my head from my hands, only to see him standing in front of us with a pristine cardboard bowl . . . and three soft tacos nestled inside. My jaw dropped.

"Did you steal those?"

He chuckled. "Don't you think we'd be running if I'd done that?" Sitting down, he held the bowl in front of me. A mouthwatering scent of garlic and pepper wafted up from the food just inches from my face. "Go on. Take one. I didn't know if you were allergic to shrimp, so I just got the chicken adobo."

Click reached out to take one of the tacos as I sat there, staring in disbelief.

"You're not a vegan or something, are you?"

"You've seen me eat meat."

"So what's the problem?"

"Are you *sure* you didn't steal these?"

"I'm sure."

"Then what did you do?"

"Asked nicely."

I turned to him with a frown. "Asked nicely?" I echoed.

"Yeah. I told the lady in the truck that I was really hungry, and that I didn't have any money. I offered to provide some entertainment to her patrons in exchange for some tacos."

"Entertainment?"

"I can sing if I have to."

In spite of the fact that I was still wary and the smell of the tacos was driving me a little wild, I couldn't help the snort of laughter that erupted from somewhere deep in my nose. "So she gave you these to shut you up and get you out of her hair?"

"Probably. I wasn't about to ask."

My fingers shook as I picked up one of the tacos, pinching the warm flour shell between my fingers. As I bit into it, I closed my eyes and let out a soft groan of pleasure.

"That good, eh?"

"Just eat your taco," I said, turning to look at him. He gave me a quick smile. "Thanks, Viktor."

"Gotta keep the hangry bunnies at bay," he said with a cheeky lift of his eyebrow as he bit into his snack. I debated giving him a swat, but decided to just enjoy the food.

CHAPTER 16

RELAPSE

Finding someone to take us to the crossroads took hours. Plenty of traffic travelled on the highway that ran through the valley, but few people seemed to be willing to take three sweaty hitchhikers with them. Out of those, some were downright scary. I vetoed the windowless panel van, even though it was driven by a good-looking guy who wasn't much older than us. The second vehicle that slowed was a rusting, two-door hatchback with a sheet of torn plastic acting as the rear window. It belched foul-smelling exhaust that made all of us cough when Viktor waved it on . . . but I was more relieved than disappointed. Something about that one hadn't felt right to me, either. Our salvation turned out to be a guy with an ancient RV that smelled so strongly of marijuana that he probably couldn't even smell Viktor. Click and I sat on the bench in the tiny kitchenette while Viktor took the passenger seat up front and kept the guy talking. Frankly, I was relieved. And Viktor liked to talk, so it was a win-win for everyone involved.

By the time we climbed out of the weedmobile, the sun was already tracing toward the west. I stared down the road that peeled off from the highway, past the locked barricade that had been set up. It looked pretty damn impassable from that side, completely blocking off the road that led into Kenyonville.

Beside me, Viktor yawned. "I can't wait to climb into bed."

"You'll have to. We've still got hours of walking ahead of us."

He let out a groan and started forward. When he reached the barricade, he just sort of stepped over it, straddling it with his long legs. Click and I both scrambled around it, getting snagged by bushes, as we'd done the previous time.

"Are you *sure* you want to do this?" I asked as we started down the road. "If you've changed your mind, tell me now. Not after we've walked for an hour."

He shook his head. "I'm sure. Aren't you?"

"No. But I don't have much of a choice. I'm kind of stuck with you."

"Hardly." The smile was evident in his voice. "You *like* us."

"I like Click," I said, casting my gaze over at the boy, who seemed to have the spring back in his step. Maybe it was the thought of reuniting with his dog.

Maybe he'd just gotten whatever bug it was out of his system. "Probably 'cause he's not always talking," I added, turning back to Viktor.

"How am I supposed to dazzle people if not with my wit? I certainly can't do it with my face."

"Your wit isn't that dazzling, either," I muttered.

"Ouch. Who needs pinkballs when you've got a tongue like that?"

My nose wrinkled as I turned to him. He burst out laughing.

"Sorry," he said. "Bad word combo."

"You think?"

—

The sun was worryingly low in the sky as we approached the checkpoint. Even though I knew what to expect this time, my heart still kicked up its rhythm. By the time I could make out the individual soldiers walking around between the structures, the streetlights that lined the road were on.

"What's our plan?" I asked, keeping my voice low in case the sound carried. "Just walk up there and let them point guns in our faces?"

"That's probably not going to happen. We're coming from the outside, remember? We're not a threat."

"Yeah, but we're walking into a restricted area. They're going to try to turn us back. What's your story when that happens?"

"How about the truth?"

"What truth?"

"Hand farts."

I rolled my eyes. "I thought we didn't have those anymore."

"We're getting closer to the Rift. Can't you feel it?"

I frowned and concentrated for a moment. Now that he mentioned it, I could feel . . . something.

"We just tell them that our powers came back."

"Viktor," I said, grabbing his arm and drawing him to a stop. He glanced at the checkpoint, then turned to look down at me. "This is a one-way trip. You get that, right?"

"Not really. What are you talking about?"

"If we show them we have pinkhands again . . . that's it. Once we go back in there, we'll never get out."

"Not unless something changes."

"We can't count on that."

He sighed. "Yeah, I get it. And I know the doc isn't going to lie for us twice. So we'll just have to make the most of it in there. For however long it takes."

"What if we spend the rest of our lives as Rifters?"

"Would that really be so bad?"

"Yes!"

With a shake of his head, he started forward again. "Shift your paradigm, Léa. The Rift Zone isn't *that* bad."

"Excuse me. You call it a heckhole all the time!"

"With affection."

"Viktor, we haven't finished discussing—" But I

didn't have a chance to finish because he suddenly blew the loudest raspberries I'd heard so far and raised his hands above his head. I gasped as I saw the pink glowing like rose-coloured fire in the deepening evening.

"Behold!" he shouted, projecting his voice like a desperate stage actor. "I have returned."

"Oh, my god," I whispered, ducking behind his body as I noticed the guards spot him. "Will you shut up? You're going to get us all shot!"

"Arms to the sides!" a male voice shouted. "Hands on your thighs." Viktor obeyed the command, looking like a rigid stick, but he kept walking.

"Viktor!" I squeaked. Click scurried forward, blocking Viktor's path.

"Move," he whispered. "Just follow my lead, okay?"

"You don't have a lead," I hissed. "You're going to get us killed!"

"Step out where we can see you," the voice commanded. I was the only one he could've possibly been talking to, so I edged to the side, warily, plastering my hands to my thighs the way we'd all done the day before.

Guards ran toward us. I wanted to run in the opposite direction, but I managed to keep my wits about me and not move. That was easier said than done, though, when they grabbed Viktor and threw him to the ground, pinning his arms to the pavement while trying to stay clear of his flaring fingers.

"Ow! Guys, I'm not—"

"Turn off your hands."

"Okay, okay. But I can't do it when you're pinning me like this."

One of them pointed his gun at the back of Viktor's head. Click let out a little grunt.

"Slowly," the man said.

"I have to sit up."

"Slowly."

Viktor moved gingerly, pulling his hands closer to his body so he could push up from the pavement. When he was on his knees, he shook his hands, sending pink sparks flying. The gun's muzzle twitched. A scream stuck in my throat. The next moment, he was pinned on the ground again, and another guard was fastening handcuffs around his wrists. They hauled him to his feet and marched him down the road toward the gate. Click and I hurried after him, but it wasn't like we had much of a choice; there were quite a few guns pointed at us, too.

Our commotion was probably the most exciting thing the soldiers had seen all week, and plenty of them came out to stare as we were marched between the portables and tents. Even Dr. Frazier came out to stand on the steps of the medical centre, squinting into the twilight.

"Hey, Doc!" Viktor said, his voice cheery despite the fact that he was being hauled—roughly—between two huge guys who didn't seem to have any sense of humour. "Looks like we relapsed."

She shook her head slowly. "Where are you taking them?"

"Back into the Zone," one of the soldiers said. He jerked Viktor's arm (rather unnecessarily, I thought) and quickened his pace.

"Wait," Dr. Frazier said. "Bring them in here."

"Protocol is to place anyone displaying symptoms of—"

"I know the protocol," she snapped. "But I just cleared these three yesterday, so I'd like to know why their symptoms have returned."

The soldiers stopped. "You *cleared* them?" one asked.

"They passed the test. I didn't have much of a choice. We can't hold unaffected kids prisoner, can we?"

The soldier looked like he wanted to say something, but Dr. Frazier didn't give him a chance. She waved her hand. "Bring them in," she said, stepping back into her portable.

Click and I followed the soldiers, who wouldn't let go of Viktor until we were all safely inside.

"You going to leave these things on?" Viktor asked incredulously as the soldiers started to leave. One of them looked at the doctor, who nodded. He unfastened the cuffs before heading for the door, not even bothering to look back. As soon as the door closed again, Dr. Frazier shook her head.

"Do I even want to know what you're doing?"

"What does it look like?" Viktor asked, rubbing his wrists.

"It looks like you're trying to break into a prison."

He dropped his hands to his sides. "It doesn't have to be." He stared at her for a long moment. "But you knew that already, didn't you?"

I sucked in a breath. She glanced at me before nodding once.

"I suspected. You're not the first people to leave—unofficially, anyway—and I've never heard of any incident involving Rift energy outside the wall."

"So you knew that if you just let everyone out of here, let them get away from the Rift . . ." My voice trailed off.

"Why do you think I signed your passes? I knew you wouldn't pose any danger once you got far enough away from the Rift. Too many lives have already been ruined by that pink monster. I didn't want any more on my conscience. Not when I had the power to do something about it." She turned to Viktor, her gaze hard. "I stuck my neck out for you. I've got the higher-ups breathing down my neck about those passes, and then you show up here, flashing your hands like—"

"If you know we're not a danger," Viktor said, "don't they?"

"Protocol." She nearly spat the word. "It doesn't matter what any of us believe or know individually. Change takes time. And a politically motivated status quo can be nearly impossible to break."

"What does *that* mean?"

"It means that the Rift and the Zone are powerful

leverage. Keeping the wall up—and all the Rifters within it—makes certain people look like they're the protectors of humanity."

"That's bullshit," I said, the words popping out before I could stop them.

"I agree. But that's the way it is." She looked at each of us, a sad expression in her eyes. "Why would you come back?"

Viktor shrugged. "There's not much for us out there. We thought we could help by coming back."

"Help?"

He nodded. "Help kids pass the test."

"I still have no idea how you managed that."

"Trade secret."

She raised an eyebrow. "Are you willing to share?"

"No offence, Doc, but you're not a Rifter."

"My scientific curiosity is piqued."

"I'm sure. But you're not exactly on our side, and I don't want to jeopardize the chances of anyone else getting out of here."

The doctor looked like she wanted to argue—after all, she *had* signed our passes the day before—but she probably realized Viktor was right. She was too old to be a Rifter. She couldn't do what we did with the Rift energy. She couldn't understand what it was like to feel that power coursing through her limbs. It had been scary, in the beginning. Uncontrolled. Uncontrollable. Viktor wasn't the only one walking around town with a scar.

At last, she shook her head, looking defeated. "I understand. But I *am* on your side, Viktor. I'm on Carrick's side. I'm on the side of every child who was left behind in there." She gestured in the direction of the Rift Zone. "I'll do what I can when they apply for exit. If you can teach them whatever trick it is that you used . . ." She looked over at me, perhaps remembering my failure. "I'll do my best, all right? I promise you that much."

"How is Carrick?" I asked, glancing toward the plastic-covered doorway at the side of the room. Her expression trembled.

"I'm keeping him comfortable. That's all I can do." She turned to Viktor as he opened his mouth. "It's all anyone can do. His injuries aren't survivable. Rift energy burns deeper than fire."

Deeper than fire. I swallowed hard as the realization of what we'd just done crashed over me. There was no turning back. We were heading back into the Rift Zone, back into the chaos, cruelty, and uncertainty of a town driven mad by an inexplicable apocalypse.

The opportunity for changing our minds was gone.

CHAPTER 17

HOMELESS

The air was cool and still as we made our way through Permanent Marc's territory in the darkness. Viktor was almost tiptoeing, trying to keep his boots from making too much noise on the deserted streets. None of us said a word; there was an unspoken agreement to keep quiet: First, so we wouldn't be heard. Second, so we could hear anyone trying to sneak up and ambush us.

We passed the high school once more, and Click drifted closer to the fence, drawn like a moth to a flame. It was hard not to be intrigued. In the darkness, we could see faint pink tendrils of energy rising up through the roof, almost like an aurora. A more intense glow came through some of the windows at the front. The sight was strangely beautiful, but I really didn't want to stop to take in the view. Without a word, Viktor veered over to where Click was standing, put a hand on his shoulder, and guided him gently back to the middle of the road.

And on we went.

By the time we reached that awful painted line on the border of the territory, all the muscles in my body felt like they were ready to tear. I was so tense, so jacked up on adrenaline, that I felt like I'd just had another shot of epi. I wanted to shout, to scream, to run down the street as fast as I could, anything to discharge some of that energy. But of course I didn't dare. I just tried to take some deep breaths while shaking my hands in front of me, as if I were shaking off pinkhands.

"You can relax now," Viktor said softly after we'd gone a few more blocks. I shook my head.

"I don't think I'll ever be able to relax again."

"Why not? It's not so bad on Niesha's turf. Well, I guess it's Katja's now. Still. Not much will have changed in thirty-six hours."

"Shit," I said, my feet shuffling to a stop. I looked up at Viktor, my eyes wide. "We didn't tell Niesha we were coming back here."

He shook his head. "She wouldn't have wanted to come, anyway. In fact, she probably would've tried to talk us out of it."

"Her dad knows where your aunt and uncle live," I said slowly, hoping he would understand what I was getting at.

"Yeah . . ."

"You said you'd be in touch. When she doesn't hear from you . . ."

He blinked. "Spit."

"Yeah."

"Son of a bunny." He turned away and heaved a deep sigh. "Aunt Marlena and Uncle Craig are going to find out I was there."

"Is it really so bad if they know you're okay?"

He whirled back around to face me. "How would your aunt and uncle feel if you came skulking around, scared your cousin, and then disappeared again, all without saying hello?"

"I don't have an aunt and uncle or a cousin," I snapped. "But if I did, I sure as hell wouldn't have played such a stupid game. You didn't want to hurt them, but you think letting them worry that their nephew is dead isn't hurtful?"

"They'll know I'm alive now."

"Yeah, they will. And your sentimental aunt will probably cry when she realizes her nephew couldn't even be bothered to let them know he's okay." My throat felt so tight, my voice was coming out in a harsh rasp. "That was a *shitty* thing to do!"

"What part?"

"All of it. This whole thing. Escaping—"

"Technically, that part was Niesha's idea."

"If you didn't want your family to know you were still alive, why did you even leave the Rift Zone at all?"

"Maybe I didn't realize what that knowledge would do to them until I saw Ramona's reaction, okay? Maybe I didn't want to make my aunt cry. Maybe I didn't want my family to have to be the object of pity, the one with *that kid*, the one with the disfigured—"

"Viktor—"

"What?" His mismatched gaze was hot as he glared at me, his eyes glistening in the glow from the street-lights. "What would you know? What can you say? You're still beautiful. Both of you are." He cast a glance at Click, who was watching his friend with wide eyes. "I'm sorry. Maybe we should've stayed out there. For your sake. But I . . ." His mouth twisted, and I suspected he was dangerously close to crying. He took a deep breath, turned on his heel, and stormed off down the sidewalk, his right hand glowing. Riftballs splattered on the wooden fence as he threw them, one after the other, his body taut with fury. Click and I exchanged a look before hurrying after him.

I didn't say anything. I didn't trust myself not to make things worse, and I didn't know if he would listen, anyway. He just kept throwing, discharging his anguish. Click and I stayed well back, letting him work out his feelings, but we followed his lead because I really wasn't sure where we were going.

I should've been able to guess, though. Soon enough, we were stepping onto the front walk of 145 Cherry Lane. Viktor stormed up the porch steps and went around the side to the window.

"Bah-dee," Click said sadly. I laid a gentle hand on his arm.

"We'll go pick him up tomorrow," I assured him. "It's kind of late. He's probably all tucked in with Dr. Bryan right now."

He frowned, but he seemed to understand. His gaze snapped up a moment later, though, as Viktor came storming around the corner of the house, his posture rigid.

"What's wrong?" I asked.

"Somebody locked the farting window." He stepped up to the front door and pounded on it, causing the pink occupancy ticket to flutter. "Come on!"

"It's not your house anymore," I said. He spun around to face me.

"Since when?"

"Um . . . since yesterday. We left. Niesha left. She's not the boss anymore."

"You think Katja moved someone in here that fast?"

"Wouldn't you? It's not a good idea to leave a cache house unoccupied."

He waved his hand at the ticket on the door.

"That's the honour system," I pointed out. "And it doesn't always mean much, especially with runners."

He glowered for a moment, then turned back to pound on the door again. It opened so fast that his fist kind of went flying into the foyer, almost striking the person standing there.

"Whoa," he breathed. "Sorry."

"It's past your bedtime," the girl said. I didn't recognize her, but that didn't mean much. I hadn't met all of Niesha's lackeys.

"Yeah. So let us in." Viktor stepped forward, but the girl moved so she was blocking the doorway. She was quite short, but she didn't seem to be intimidated by Viktor's looming stature at all.

"Are you kidding? You're supposed to be living it up on the outside."

"Sure. Caviar and filet mignon, right?"

She narrowed her eyes. Behind her, the house had a warm glow, something that seemed achingly familiar. "Look, Viktor, I don't know what you think you're doing, but you left. You don't get to just waltz back in here. This isn't your house."

"It never was," he said. "It was Niesha's."

"Yeah, and Niesha left. Katja's in charge now."

"We know that. So? What's the problem? Katja likes me. *Everybody* likes me."

The girl snorted. "Ego, much?"

"Are you denying it?"

"I could take you or leave you. But you're not the issue."

This seemed to take him aback. "Huh?"

"She is." The girl pointed out the door . . . and straight at me.

I took a step back. "What did I do?" I squeaked.

"Oh, I don't know," she said. But her tone made it

totally obvious that she did know. She frowned as she peered out the door as if searching for something. "Where *is* Niesha?"

"She decided to stay in Goldvale," Viktor said. He braced one hand on the doorframe and leaned forward. "What does that have to do with Léa?"

"What do you think?"

"I honestly don't know."

The girl rolled her eyes. "Katja was in love with her, okay?"

Viktor pulled his head back in surprise. "Who? Léa?"

"No, dumbass. Niesha." She turned to glare at me. "And who took Niesha away?"

"Wait a minute," I said, holding up my hands. "I didn't do anything."

"Leaving was Niesha's idea," Viktor added. "Léa didn't even want to leave at first."

The girl shrugged and grasped the edge of the door. "Whatever. The point is, Niesha's gone. And Katja's pissed. If I let her"—she angled her chin in my direction—"in here, and Katja finds out . . ."

"What?" Viktor asked. "Katja's, like, eighteen. You think she's going to have a bunny-fit like a middle-schooler because she's jealous of another girl?"

"I'm just trying to protect her. Not that you'd get it, Viktor, but some of us have real friends that we care about."

"Excuse me? I have friends."

"No, you have people who tolerate you." She started

to push the door closed. "I'm not going to hurt Katja. So if you're as friendly as you say you are, you'll figure out a way to help those two." She tilted her chin toward me and Click. "But it won't be here," she said, and slammed the door.

"Fart," Viktor muttered. He turned to face us as the lock clunked.

"Is any of that true?" I asked.

"I have *friends.*"

I shook my head. "No. About Niesha and Katja."

He sighed and clomped down the porch steps. "I don't know. Niesha's bi, but I don't know how she felt about Katja. I guess we know how Katja felt about her, though."

"What about me?"

"What about you?"

"Was Niesha . . . I mean, did she . . ." My words caught in my throat.

"Did she have a thing for you?"

I shrugged.

"Not that I know of. And, even if she had, she wouldn't have let you know. She had kind of a policy against that sort of thing."

"I know. She told me."

He reached up to tighten his ponytail. "She doesn't have to worry about that now. Out there." His gaze was distant as he stared back toward the street.

"I'm sorry," I said miserably. "I just keep fucking things up."

He looked down at me with a frown. "How so?"

"First, I couldn't get the hang of redirecting the Rift energy, so you had to wait to attempt the escape. Then I failed the test. And now we have no home."

"That's not your fault." He glanced back over his shoulder at the house. "That's just a minion with an overdeveloped and misguided sense of loyalty."

"Viktor, we're *homeless*."

He shrugged. "Kenyonville is full of unoccupied houses."

"Yeah, and after three years, most of those have had the walls peed on and the cupboards shat in."

"So we ally ourselves with another boss."

"No." I shook my head. "No way."

"They're not all batspit like Permanent Marc. I hear C-Roy isn't bad."

"He isn't bad. He isn't great, either."

He folded his arms. "Well, what do you suggest? You want to go it alone?"

"That's a great way to starve." I shook my head. "We'll have to do odd jobs for the bosses, at least, if we want to eat."

"What about your friend the vet?"

"He's probably only got enough food for himself. I'm not going to ask him to share."

"Who's the boss in that part of town?"

"Ryver Wells, I think."

"Ever worked for her?"

I shook my head.

"Well, the fact that the vet hasn't starved to death bodes well for us."

"What do you mean?"

"Ryver obviously realizes the benefits of having skilled adults around. Which means she's smarter than most of the other bosses in town."

"The bar isn't very high."

He grunted in amusement. "I won't tell Niesha you said that."

"Yeah, you won't. Because she's not here." *We are*, I almost added, but decided the obvious didn't need to be stated.

Viktor stepped onto the grass, into the shadow of the overgrown rhododendron, and sat down. Click joined him. But I stayed standing, hugging myself against the cool night air.

"What are you doing?" I asked.

"We'll figure things out tomorrow," he said. "After we pick up Buddy. Okay?"

Click gave him a thumbs up, his expression bright.

"We might as well stay here for the night," Viktor went on, turning back to me. "It's safer than wandering around out there."

He was probably right, though I hated to admit it. Still feeling like our shitty accommodations for the night were my fault, I went and sat next to him, staring miserably at the patchy grass.

"Cold?" he asked. I shook my head and tugged my jacket around me. Without a word, he scooted closer and put his arm around my shoulders. Click crawled to my other side and did the same. My first instinct was to pull away from both of them.

But then I realized I didn't want to.

"Things always look better in the morning," Viktor said. "Well, maybe not my face. But—"

"Stop," I whispered. "Don't."

"Okay." He rested his cheek against my hair and gave my shoulders a squeeze. "You're all right."

I wasn't sure why he chose that particular moment to say that particular thing. But I was glad he had . . . because it was exactly what I needed to hear.

Maybe it was what we both needed to hear.

ALSO BY NISSA HARLOW

Two Between Worlds
The Last Minute
No Such Thing
Elements of Mind: The Complete Quartet

<u>Generation Rift</u>
Nothing Close to Home
Escape From the Zone
So Lost Are the Foes
All the Scars of Hope

ABOUT
THE AUTHOR

Nissa Harlow wanted to be a writer from the time she was a small child, but it took a while before she finally did anything about it. In the meantime, she worked as a volunteer day-camp counsellor, a movie extra, and a digital-photo editor. She even once worked on a conveyor belt in a chocolate factory (which was as stressful—and delicious—as it sounds).

These days, she lives in British Columbia, Canada and writes stories about friendship, love, and healing, all embellished with a touch of the fantastic.

www.ingramcontent.com/pod-product-compliance
Lightning Source LLC
Chambersburg PA
CBHW051226210726
48290CB00003B/814